DEADLY PROBABILITIES

D.L. KOONTZ

DEADLY PROBABILITIES By DL Koontz

Published by BRIMSTONE FICTION, LLC.

1440 W. Taylor St.

Suite #447, Chicago, IL

60607

ISBN: 978-1-846758-34-7

Cover design by Elaina Lee www.Forthemusedesigns.com

Interior Design by Meaghan Burnett—www.meaghanburnett.com

Available in print and ebook from your local bookstore, online, or from the publisher at: www.BrimstoneFiction.com

For more information on this book and the author, visit: www.dlkoontz.com

Brought to you by the creative team at Brimstone Fiction : Meaghan Burnett, Rowena Kuo & Jessie Andersen

Library of Congress Cataloging-in-Publication Data

Koontz, DL

Deadly Probabilities / DLKoontz 1st ed.

Printed in the United States of America

To Johanna Traverso, my lovely daughter-in-law and daughter at heart.

ACKNOWLEDGMENTS

I offer my thanks to the following people:

Meaghan Burnett, publishing and marketing guru, who set this romantic suspense three-book series in motion and who has been there every step of the way.

Joseph Roberson, my wonderful husband, who encourages me to write over cleaning, cooking, and just about every one of the thousands of tasks necessary to operate a cattle ranch. Who wouldn't love a guy like that?

Matthew Traverso, my son, sounding board for all life throws at me, and my own personal IT department when technology overwhelms me (which is a bit too often). And, to Johanna (Joie) Traverso, for her patience when I call my IT department.

Mike Hargrove, my source for all things related to police and detective work. You've helped me out of several corners I've written myself into.

X, who wants to remain anonymous, for guidance on all questions pertaining to federal law enforcement agencies and bureaus and the military. You know who you are.

Cynthia Parker, my amazing friend, for believing in me and always encouraging me.

Danny Harrell, for being my biggest cheerleader and for your faith that my books should be born.

Darlene Reighard, Brenda Orndorff, and Mandy Feight, my sister-cousins, who have often implied that writing books isn't the worst way I could spend my time.

The Jacques family, for showing me just how incredible the view from a mountain house in Smithsburg, MD could be.

My friends in West Virginia (and portions of Pennsylvania) who still enjoy mountain vistas even as I let love lead me to the flatlands of southeast Georgia. In my heart I still sing *Take Me Home, Country Roads*.

All the people from my journalism days, for helping me realize that newspapers come in black and white, but people come in all shades of gray. Those experiences helped me see that journalists and news stories never represent the whole of a person or the whole of the truth, instead shedding light on only one small aspect. That, then, helped me close the wrong door on journalism and open the right door to fiction.

Jessie Andersen, for her excellent suggestions and edits and for making me believe she enjoys reading my books.

All the wonderful people at Brimstone Fiction who had a part in this book: Meaghan Burnett, Rowena Kuo & Jessie Andersen.

My writing friends at The Light Brigade.

All the new friends I'll make due to this book who choose to follow me on Facebook and Instagram. If you're optimistic and light-hearted, then come ruminate and laugh with me while we enjoy life's journey.

As always, to God be the greatest glory.

PRELUDE

He clicked off the cell phone, sinking back in his chair, his deep restlessness subsiding as a smile played at the corners of his mouth.

An explosion. That's what the caller had said.

He stroked a pensive finger down the cup of his lukewarm coffee, thinking.

What timing! This could finally be it.

His chance.

This could change his life. Restore what he'd lost. Escalate him to what was his due, to where he should have been all along—his wallet lined with cash, his skin touching only finest cashmere and silk, his body waking each morning with an enviable view of where the bay struggles against the ocean, and driving the sweet ride of that Maserati he'd been eyeing.

It might even remove that recurring anger that curled inside his belly and inched up his throat until he felt he might choke on it.

Up to now, his lot in life had been marked by an unfairness, the kind he deserved to be plucked from hurriedly, not inched from after more years of delivering platitudes and praise to idiots that didn't deserve it.

All those people who said he couldn't ... that he was deficient ... too coarse ... not worthy.

He'd show them.

He trembled at the sheer joy spreading through his core.

One mere explosion.

Take a metal industrial drum and arrange for it to—*whoops!*—turn over. A simple spill. Those happened all the time, didn't they?

Add a spark, the smallest touch of fire—indisputably mankind's single, greatest invention, after all—and the result?

Kaboom!

He divined great things ahead for his future, the thought causing a palpable chill to run through his core, a beam of boyish pleasure to morph his face.

Oh, what respect he would command then!

To celebrate, he pulled one of his many illegal Cuban cigars from the jewel-encrusted humidor he'd won in a poker game. He rarely smoked his expensive stogies indoors. Stale odors reminded him too much of his upbringing, a past he'd turned his back on long ago. A childhood made up of the sounds of backstreet brawls, the smells of frying and ill-functioning sewers, and the views of loaded clothes lines filled with tattered garments and towels hanging high above the streets and flapping in the wind like flags of defeat. He didn't want his new environment to be stamped with any odor or visual that suggested anything except freshness and possibility.

However, this was a special occasion.

His occasion.

And he wanted to celebrate it alone with a pricey smoke he'd seen the affluent smoke in countless photos.

Solitude suited him best anyway. Always had ... at least, after his mother died when he was only six. After that, his alcoholic father had showered him with too much heavy-handed attention. He had never been able to do anything right to please the man, and he'd grown tired of a father who should have loved and protected him instead of calling him stupid and worthless. Sure, he'd had his sister to run interference from time to time, but the old man's slaps and punches had left their mark, both physically and mentally. Their father had left their mark on his sister too, but it would end there, he determined as he patted a cylinder of ash into his brass ashtray.

A crackling crash of thunder sounded, interrupting his thoughts, and he turned in his chair to look out the fifth-story window where rain pattered loudly. A breeze clutched at the many awnings and flags in the cityscape.

Cigar in hand, he stood and moved to the window, flinging it open. The energy in the air tingled his skin. His heart raced as the hair on his arms and neck rose, prickling with electricity, causing him to shake with an unfamiliar delight.

This storm was his, he was certain—apropos at this time—to mark the moment in his life when he had been fueled with new energy.

In the thunder, he could almost hear the whack of a gauntlet thrown down before him, a challenge for him to grab what he was owed and run with it.

He paused to look out at the city, but in his imagination, he had moved beyond this particular view, destined as he was—he was certain —to a view from a higher, loftier perch. Below him, everywhere, traffic moved, swerved, maneuvered its way in haste. Shopkeepers rolled up iron gates, customers milled into the local coffee shop, and a homeless man searched through a garbage can. None of these people had his wherewithal, his drive, his abilities. How in the world could society dictate he wait in line behind these people and vie equally for parking spaces? How could they use the same sidewalks and escalators, take the same taxis and shuttles, and secure the best tables in restaurants as him?

He turned from the window but couldn't sit. Back and forth he paced and puffed, ignoring the incoming breeze as it wreaked havoc in the room. He was still shaking.

Still thinking.

One thing that crystallized in his mind's eye with utter certainty was that his life had been decisively changed with that call.

One simple, easy, inconsequential explosion.

He grinned, triumphant. Turning back to the window, cigar draping from the side of his mouth, he looked out upon the world, pointed his index finger, thumb raised, and pretended to shoot—his version of having the last word, of closing an issue his way.

CHAPTER ONE

Crowded. Noisy. Musty.

Exhaust fumes. Blasting horns. Intense people scurrying every direction, their frenetic pursuits stifled by horrendous traffic, and conversations interrupted by shrill sirens.

Welcome back to Washington D.C., Ann McCarthy mused as she rounded the corner from the Archives-Navy Memorial metro exit to the Pennsylvania Avenue building housing her office.

Charles Dickens had dubbed the country's nerve center as the City of Magnificent Intentions.

More like the City of Grand Delusions. After twelve years, Ann's love affair with the Capital city had long since expired. She found it increasingly hard to leave her peaceful weekends in rural West Virginia. But she'd made a pledge to her terminally ill mother, and she intended to keep it.

Eighteen more months.

Then she could leave this stifling metropolis and this work for good. She didn't care if she never owned another briefcase or power suit for as long as she lived.

Without breaking her well-honed, don't-mess-with-me stride, Ann fished in her purse to find the access badge to her building. She looked up in time to see a tornado of leather on a bicycle rush at her.

In the next second there was a blur of sky and building peaks then she sprawled on the concrete, a thick form wearing dark sunglasses and a black ball cap staring down at her.

Lost in a momentary stupor, her mind flashed back several years to a similar moment when she'd ended up hugging concrete. That had been right after her ex-boyfriend Aiden hit her. *For the last time.*

"Geez, Lady, you okay?" The biker's voice boomed, his gaze assessing passersby as though more concerned about them than her. "You oughta' watch where you're going." He supported her arm to help her up then draped the long straps of her purse and briefcase over her shoulder. Patting her arm twice, he leaned close to her ear and whispered in a menacing snarl: "Keep out of it. Or next time will be for real."

The hair on Ann's neck prickled at the warning and her heart knocked against her rib cage. "Wait, what?" Startled, she attempted to switch her focus from standing upright, brushing dirt from her navy suit, and adjusting her load, to what the guy mumbled. She did a full 360-degree turn, looking for him.

He was nowhere in sight.

In the fall, a lock of her long dark hair had broken free from the up-do she'd styled so carefully that morning. With a sigh, she pushed it from her eyes and took a tenuous step. All body parts moved as they should, although she felt like a slumping puppet whose strings had been severed.

She shifted her attention to inspect her belongings. Purse, check. Briefcase, check. Watch, check. She thrust a hand to check the jewelry at her neck and ears. Check and check.

Amazing. It had been an accident. Not a theft. The guy's bullying comment must have been his grousing way of warning her not to get the police involved. She shook her head at the absurdness. Why would he think she might raise a ruckus over an innocent sidewalk collision? Besides, she hadn't even gotten a good look at him. She couldn't identify him if her life depended on it.

Perhaps D.C. should be called the City of Quirky Surprises.

Then again, not one person had stopped to help her. *No surprise there.*

She looked around to see who might have witnessed her unfortunate encounter with the cyclist. A group of teenage tourists dressed in school uniforms squabbled and laughed as they made their way down the street, a bus screeched to its customary stop near the corner, a dog walker wrestled the leashes of five dogs to maneuver them around a newspaper kiosk where the owner thumped newspapers into piles. From every direction people walked, hurried, jaywalked between vehicles, and dashed to their destinations, all appearing oblivious to her and what she'd just experienced.

She needed to get out of this town.

Once past the yawning guard at the entrance of the building, she joined the throngs of people scrambling for the elevators as though split seconds of waiting would destroy their schedules for days.

On the seventh floor, Ann squeezed through a wall of suits and exited, crashing smack-dab into the side of a blonde woman attempting to get on. Nothing unusual, given that people often got off on the wrong floor at this time of the morning. Shuffling with the crowd often resulted in disorientation.

What *was* unusual, however, was the woman's reaction. Her cheeks were flamed with anger and her hands fisted until she eyed Ann. In an instant, her face drained of color and she jerked up her purse to cover her face.

"Tracy?" Ann asked, turning to watch the panicked woman disappear into the crowded elevator. "I didn't know you made—" The doors closed, and Ann finished to herself, "—deliveries." She cocked her head. That was Tracy from the lobby coffee shop. Wasn't it? Why would she act so aloof?

Ann took a calming breath. If she wasn't careful, this town would run her over before she could wave it goodbye for good.

Stark reminder to toughen up because she was back in D.C. again.

She crossed the marbled receiving area toward the front desk, as the young receptionist answered the demanding phone.

"CRS. Claire speaking. May I help you?" Pause. "Yes, that stands for Corporate Response Specialists." Pause. "Uh-huh. Please hold while I transfer." She pushed a couple buttons, hung up, and stood to greet Ann.

"Good morning," Claire said, offering two call slips. "Webb's running behind. Just now leaving Philly. And the rep from the Department of Energy called to thank you for the report. How was your weekend?"

Ann sighed. "As usual, too relaxing and pleasant and—"

Voices sounded from the office of her partner Sam Bromberg. Acerbic voices. The distance from office to receiving desk prevented Ann from discerning what was said, but the discordant timbre signaled a heated difference of opinion.

Startled, Ann flicked her gaze to the office and back to Claire as tension shot down her back.

"Oh, yeah," Claire shrugged a shoulder. "Sam is talking to that handsome guy from LubeRoyal."

Ann bit her lip. "Do you know what's—"

A thud sounded, like that of a fist smacking a desk. Then came: "Yes, now!"

At least those two words were loud and clear.

The thunderous voice continued. "We have a crisis underway! I have a dead employee, and your firm is looking more suspicious by the minute. So, call this guy McCarthy and tell him to get his butt here pronto. Then we'll discuss who at CRS may be in the business of sabotage and murder." The man's baritone voice had escalated until his last word echoed through the reception area.

Ann squared her shoulders and hurried to Sam's office.

Sam and the owner of the voice faced each other, bodies swelled like duelists taking each other's measure. The stranger stood a good five inches over Sam. She could see why Claire dubbed him "handsome." He had a blue-collar physique stuffed into a white-collar suit. His chiseled chin and muscular outline were softened by intense blue eyes and impeccable tailoring, but his persona reeked of heated testosterone.

Focus.

Ann nodded at Sam as she parked her bags on a side table. Step-

4

ping to the stranger, she thrust out a hand. "I'm Ann McCarthy. My butt is here, so what can I do for you?"

Sam sighed a sound of relief, "Ann, this is Logan Kassell. He's with—"

"LubeRoyal," she said, looking back to Logan and ignoring the odd sensation that quivered through her when she gripped his muscular hand. *Was that Burberry men's cologne?* The man oozed quality.

But she knew this suit type. It was the kind she vowed to stay away from when it came to her personal life. She wouldn't repeat that mistake again. "You're Corporate Security Director for LubeRoyal. Located at their world headquarters in Baltimore."

Logan raised an eyebrow but said nothing. He studied her a long moment, his gaze flicking from her Italian leather shoes to her Armani suit. His lips twitched. She suspected that some deep-seated training to be civil warred with his determination to spew his anger. Was it her choice of attire he disapproved of, or the fact she was a woman?

"You're McCarthy?" His voice harbored a hint of dismay. Or skepticism? Perhaps both. And that undertone of anger was still there.

Ahh. He had expected McCarthy to be a man. She couldn't fault him for his pre-conceived notions. Crisis management was a male-dominated field, after all.

"Call me Ann."

Logan hitched a thumb at Sam. "He said you're the on-duty partner this week?"

"That's correct."

"We had an explosion. Early this morning. Your firm recently signed a contract to develop crisis plans for us."

"I'm aware of our contracts, Mr. Kassell."

"According to the agreement—"

"We're obligated to help you tackle any unfortunate events that occur until we've completed a turn-key program such that your company can handle corporate emergencies on its own," she finished for him. "Is that what you had in mind?"

She watched as he coddled his agitation behind curled lips. *Was that a smirk?*

"Yes, that about covers it." He stared at her, blue eyes intent.

She folded her arms, shifted her stance. "You came here directly rather than calling? That's forty-five minutes wasted."

He arched a brow. "I was in town. Attended a weekend seminar with the EPA."

Ann wasn't surprised. Proximity was why she, Sam, and their third partner, Webb Hollis, had headquartered the firm in the Capital. Washington D.C. was a strategic location for a consulting business specializing in crisis management. Clients trekked to the capital to meet with regulators and attorneys. While there, they received updates on ever-increasing safety and security legislation that applied to their industry. Generally, it was a logical next step to meet with CRS or one of their competitors to secure a contract for corporate-wide crisis response plans.

Ann took pride in the services her firm delivered. With the job came money, travel, prestige, and a wardrobe allowance—all heady and exciting. It just wasn't the way she wanted to spend the rest of her life. Her family's West Virginia farm and a simpler life were calling.

But her mother was counting on her. So, this was her life right now, and despite the agitated vibes she felt from this man, she needed to establish trust and inspire confidence.

"What caused the explosion?" she asked.

He huffed and rubbed a line between his eyebrows. "Do you even know much about our company and what we do?" His voice suggested doubt; his demeanor forced tolerance.

Ann straightened her spine but ignored the undertone of an insult. "You're a $6.2 billion specialty company and global supplier of chemical technologies. Including additives for engine oils and industrial lubricants, as well as additives for gasoline and diesel fuel. You're also a producer of advanced specialty polymers used in hundreds of products. Twenty-three locations. Seven-thousand employees worldwide. Now, please tell me what happened."

She could see Sam's smug smile from where he stood behind Logan. He loved it when she rattled off facts like this to clients. It generally made her, and therefore the firm, sound skilled and capable, when really all it reflected was her keen memory and research skills. They'd always been an asset, especially back when she worked as a news reporter.

Logan twisted his lips as though surprised to find himself impressed. "The operators blended a mix last evening. A rush job for Aplex Corporation. The company's in Richmond and couldn't get their specialized tankers here until later today. Our operators stored it in the south tank area overnight. For some reason, it ruptured in the early hours of the morning. Xylene poured everywhere. Ignited. Killed one of our guys."

Ann cringed as sadness poured over her. "How awful." She looked away and said a silent prayer for the man's family. Her throat tightened, and she pulled herself together, making eye contact. She never lost her composure in front of clients, especially one she'd just met. "You need to take his family aside and protect them from the news media. They deserve a chance to mourn in peace."

"They're taken care of, and we're not releasing the name until the family gives the okay."

She nodded her approval. "How did this happen?"

"Still being investigated," he said as he flung his hands wide in a who-knows gesture. "Maybe a faulty drum, or a fracture in a transfer hose. But I can't believe that would cause such a severe rapture. My staff is still investigating."

"How bad is it?"

"We don't know the extent of the damage. Several fire departments responded. And of course, the news media." He scowled. "Collier, my head of grounds security, said one radio report already suggested neglect, and another, human error. I'm waiting for his callback."

As though on que, Logan's cell phone sounded. He read the display. "That's him. Excuse me." He stepped out of the office.

Through the open door, Ann could see him pace as he talked on the phone. She turned to Sam and watched him clap his hands together, rubbing them with the sort of exuberance he might have exhibited if he learned he'd won the lottery.

"Ka-ching," he whispered.

Angered, Ann shushed him. It was obvious Sam had savored the exchange with Logan as though it were an aphrodisiac, a stimulant that brought their firm closer to being the kings of crisis response he wanted them to be. His arrogance was unparalleled at times. Lately, it had grown worse and begun to disgust Ann.

Sam smirked. "You know what this means," he said, a smile lingering on his lips, his words as smooth as silk sheets.

Yes, she knew too well what it meant.

It meant they would once again prosper from a company's pain.

It meant CRS could bill at double the hourly rate until the crisis was under control.

It meant more notoriety for the firm because this crisis would be broadcast nationwide, perhaps internationally.

And it meant that once again, the unfortunate, and uncanny, timing. Had CRS already developed LubeRoyal's crisis plans, the chemical company would be perfectly situated to handle the response on its own. But caught without plans, as it was now, it would flounder, probably suffer severe economic loss and a tarnished reputation.

Ann fixed him with a glare. "Sam, it means you better not let him see your pleasure at their pain." Her voice was tart. "They're a good company, composed of good people. They don't deserve what's happened. And let's not forget that someone died! We're going to do everything we can to close this out for them ASAP."

"Yeah, yeah," Sam waved it off with a flick of his hand.

"Why was Mr. Kassell so angry when I arrived? What happened before I got here?"

Sam turned away from her to fidget at a stack of papers on his desk. "He's just irked about the situation. Doesn't know where to direct his anger."

From the doorway, Logan cleared his throat and stepped back into the office.

"Collier said it's a circus." He turned to Ann. "I have to leave. Now."

She met his gaze. "My team and I will be ten minutes behind you in our company van. We keep suitcases packed at the office for extended stays."

"Then I'll see you there," he said with some asperity as he turned back toward the door to leave.

"Wait, take my card." Ann hurried to her purse and fossicked through it. "You and I can talk strategy by cell phone on the way."

She pulled out her card case, and with it came a small wire she didn't recognize. Confused, she yanked the remainder of it out, holding it high like she might hold a dead mouse. Attached at the other end was a hunk of modeling clay, molded into a crude shape about the size of a fist. Stuck to one end was a small stopwatch and a string.

For a heartbeat, she stared at it, waiting for her brain to supply some explanation.

Necessary logic.

Anything.

Panic bloomed and a tiny cry escaped her lips as icy dread swirled in her gut. "Wh...What is this?"

Logan reached for it. Lifted it close. "A fake bomb."

"Fake?" She choked out the word. "How do you know?"

"It's empty. Just a mold." He turned it over and pointed into one end. "See, it's just a hollow shell of clay. If it were real, none of us would be alive right now to discuss it." In a demanding tone, he asked, "Who's had access to this bag?"

Ann felt the color drain from her face. "I don't know ... I commuted on the crowded Metro. It could have been anyone." That quickly, the biker and his threat flashed in her memory. She reached out to steady herself using Sam's desk. *Stay calm. Don't show weakness. People use it to their advantage.* "We ... we should call the police."

"We should." Logan agreed, a muscle ticking in his jaw. "But we're not going to." He tucked the device in the lower right pocket of his suit jacket, grabbed her purse and briefcase, and put an arm behind her back, steering her toward the door. "Let your team bring your suitcase. You're coming with me. *Now.*"

❧

LOGAN STEERED his LubeRoyal company car onto the Capital Beltway. They would stay on this road for two miles before exiting onto Route 295, taking them to Baltimore in about forty minutes.

Morning sun buttered the budding trees in Greenbelt Park as they drove by, and it reminded him of an innocent drawing a preschooler might sketch.

If only life were that simplistic. Two more years and he'd be able to live that quiet life he craved.

He glanced at his fidgeting guest in the passenger seat. Watched her smooth the skirt at her knees as though the simple action would straighten out the discomfort in the car. A conflict of emotions seemed to be vying for control within her. They'd been in the car six minutes, and she hadn't relaxed. Or said a word. Yet clearly, there was much to discuss. In fact, the air in the vehicle was aswarm with unspoken things. If it would work, he'd open the window to let some out.

Was she worried about that phony explosive she'd discovered? She had recoiled as though it were a poisonous viper. Or was she mad at how he refused to take time to call the police, maneuvering her away instead? Now that he thought about it, her reaction had been about equal to both. Was any of it an act? Was she cunning enough to be involved in sabotaging his company for the sake of building up her own?

If not, then she might be in danger. The device may have been counterfeit, but his gut told him the threat was all too real. The timing alone—coming on the heels of the LubeRoyal incident—was too odd to be ignored.

Her reaction to the device had seemed genuine. If she wasn't behind it, then who was? Was there any connection between this threat and what had happened at his company that morning? Was he putting her in more danger by bringing her to LubeRoyal?

He needed to keep an eye on her, but he wasn't sure whether it was to expose or protect her. No offense to cops, but he knew calling them would take too long, merely to end up unresolved anyway. The concern was in Baltimore, not D.C.

Wasn't it?

But what was it about this woman—this female with the most intriguing raven hair and eyes he'd ever seen—that forced him to work harder to focus on what she said than how she looked?

And her hutzpah! Impressive. Particularly the way she'd entered the office, despite obviously having heard his unfortunate exchange with Bromberg. She'd looked him in the eye, knowing full well he had expected her to be a man. She'd stood firm like a drawn saber, ready to take what he thrust at her.

He shook his head. *Where was that coming from?*

He'd better shake off these thoughts, and quickly. In his experience, women of money and power who worked in D.C. did not appreciate a man showing testosterone-driven concern. Instead of welcoming it, they seemed to resent it. Besides, she wasn't his type at all. Women like her thrived in complexity and complication.

Still, she might be innocent, and he hadn't meant to be gruff at her office. He wanted to offer the benefit of the doubt, to believe she and her company were innocent.

Scuttlebutt around the industry was that CRS provided excellent services. However, twice this past year CRS's new clients mysteriously experienced a crisis after signing for services but *before* CRS could start developing those plans.

That morning, his company became number three.

Sure, it could be coincidence. It could also mean someone at CRS had ulterior motives to bring in mega money. When he'd returned to Bromberg's office after taking his call from Collier, he had caught their heated gazes ricocheting like billiard balls. Some sort of frenzied communication took place in his absence, and he wondered what it was.

Too bad he had been out of town when the contract had been awarded and signed. If he'd had a chance to meet that Bromberg character first ...

"Look," Logan said, "sorry to rush you from the office, but time is of the essence."

He watched as she lifted her chin, becoming taller in her seat. She looked at him with such a resolute stare that he found it somewhat disarming. Was she trying to ascertain his sincerity?

"It was a little ... abrupt, yes," she said. "But you're the client, and we aim to serve you as best we can."

Despite her calm, practiced answer, he detected an undertone of annoyance, a struggle to remain professional. He caught her hand shaking as she lifted it to push a wayward strand of hair from her face.

"That contraption you pulled from your bag? What you don't know," he said slowly, simultaneously focusing on getting the correct exit to 295, "is that during my call with Collier, I learned parts of an explosive device were found at the accident site. The one planted on you was fake, but it's looking probable that the pieces found at my company were part of a real one. Were they alike? It's too early to be sure. I haven't seen the other one. It could be coincidence, given that this is the most popular home-made explosive there is. A YouTube video will show you in seconds how to produce one."

Ann sucked in a quick burst of air and jerked her wide brown eyes to look at him again. He noted confusion mixed with fear reflected there. "What does that mean? And why me?"

Her movement had loosened that strand of hair to cross her face again. He wrenched his gaze to the road, resisting the urge to tuck it back in place. Better not think about what those long tresses would look like when set free of that binding. Wasn't it enough that her herbal scent invaded his car?

Logan tightened his hold on the steering wheel as though a firmer grip translated to getting a better hold on his thoughts. *Was she innocent?* His suspicions argued not to be pushed aside so lightly.

"It means we need to take these threats seriously." He maneuvered the car around a slow-moving eighteen-wheeler hauling new cars. "This explosion was no accident. More like sabotage. And there is always the possibility someone from one of our companies may be involved."

Her jaw dropped. "What? No. My firm is in the business of helping companies, not destroying them."

He firmed his mouth, determined not to respond. Best to think before he spoke. Buying time, he released a pair of sunglasses from his visor and donned them to filter the May sun's glare.

A taut silence fell. There was no sound but traffic passing by.

Stalling would get them nowhere. He may as well confront her. "How well do you know Bromberg?"

"Sam?" She cocked her head. "Well enough to know he's not a murderer if that's what you're implying." Her tone was barbed.

"The death may have been an accident. An unfortunate result of a different plan."

Her gaze drifted as if she were studying something in her mind and choosing her words with care. "I admit Sam's a little ... self-serving, but he doesn't have drastic intentions like that. Besides, his wife is independently wealthy. Why would he bother?"

Logan thought about her answer. Of course, she would defend the guy. They were business partners. She had to protect her company and her investment in it.

He pondered his next words. He didn't want to sound like a prude, but as a child of the foster care system, he was repulsed by people who didn't appreciate their families. "When I arrived, your receptionist waved me into his office. I don't think she knew Bromberg already had company. He was sharing an impassioned exchange with a blonde that didn't look anything like the woman in the family picture on his desk."

Ann's eyes pulled together to glare at him. "An *impassioned exchange*. What does that mean?"

Had he touched a nerve? Stoked a jealousy? "Intense. Maybe heated. Like they both had a personal investment in the conversation. And each other."

She opened her mouth as though to say something then seemed to think better of it. Instead, she shrugged. "I thought I saw Tracy from the coffee shop leaving our offices. She seemed ... out of sorts."

He chuckled, perhaps a little too derisively. "A heated discussion about coffee and donuts? I don't think so."

She turned her gaze from him. "I can't be certain who it was. Probably an old friend."

"What about your other partner. Webb Hollis, right? How well do you know him?"

"Webb?" She jerked her gaze back, eyes flaring. "Don't even go there. You will never meet a nicer, more trustworthy man."

Logan frowned at the conviction in her tone. And at her obstinance. Her own logic was making her the target of his suspicions. "What about you? Any significant other that wants to help you excel?" He noticed she wore no wedding ring.

She crossed her arms, and anger escaped through a sigh. He sensed she was tolerating his questions because she had to. After all, she was in his company car, and he was her client.

"First, Mr. Kassell," she said rather acerbically, "if you're running through a list of suspects, then you ought to look at your own organization. A company of your size could have" —she ticked off suggestions using her fingers— "overzealous investors, angry competitors, unhappy neighbors, anxious suppliers, disgruntled employees and their families, and disappointed customers."

Logan winced. She wasn't wrong. Especially the way Jonathan Tate handled operations.

Her clipped words continued, filling the car like zinging bullets. "Not that it's any of your business, but no, there is no one special right now. Outside of work, my life is ... dull. My brother and his wife live in Minneapolis, run a bakery, and are expecting their first child. Hardly the type to bomb companies. My parents were professors at West Virginia University. When they retired, they pursued mission work in Zimbabwe. After Dad had a heart attack six years ago, they moved home. Dad passed away a year later and Mom now is battling lymphoma and living on the family estate, a nonworking farm. No crops, no animals. I spend weekends in West Virginia with her, and I share an apartment through the week with two roommates who think that living on the wild side consists of ordering in a meat-laden pizza. That," she heaved a sigh and looked at him pointedly, "is the gist of my life."

Was she issuing a challenge?

He grimaced. His suspicions had faded a bit when she mentioned her missionary parents. And, meaty pizza? His kind of meal. He'd have to ask her about that later. "You get along well with your roommates? You trust them?"

Ann bristled. "I wouldn't live with them if I didn't trust them, Mr. Kassell." Her tone said she was miffed but was likely indulging his questions and suspicions because he was the client.

She leaned forward and pulled a pen and tablet from the briefcase at her feet. "I should be asking the same questions of you, about your company and your life."

His life? He and his half-sister Ginny were foster kids, so family could be ruled out. Besides, Ginny was only eleven, too young to have enemies of this proportion. He intended to keep it that way if it was the last thing he ever did.

But there was that heated exchange he'd had with his platoon mate Dash Bower. Logan had long suspected Dash suffered from PTSD. When he witnessed Dash brutally slamming his wife against a wall, Logan had intervened to protect her. Sadly, as with many domestic abuse victims, Dash's wife afterward denied the incident ever occurred. Next thing Logan knew, he was the one being tagged with PTSD, for excessive force against Dash!

The situation had provided his Uncle Jonathan—his dead biological mother's brother—with the perfect opportunity to seize control over Ginny, and in so doing, Logan too. Tate had labeled his proposed arrangement a bargain. Logan had called it what it was: manipulation and blackmail. Jonathan Tate's conditions had been clear: Logan had to agree to leave his carpentry business to head LubeRoyal's security for eight years. During that time, Tate would be legal guardian to Ginny, but she could live with Logan. If Logan faltered on the eight years or failed to obey his uncle during that time, Tate would tell authorities that the PTSD concern was legit. If Logan served all eight years, Tate would sign over guardianship to Logan. That was six years ago. Two more years to go before Ginny would be free of an uncle who, at best, was callous and distant to her.

Logan rubbed his neck fleeing the thoughts of his uncle. No time for that now. The topic at hand was potential enemies, and he could not in all sincerity rule out Dash. The last Logan had heard, Dash had begun drinking heavily, lost his job and his wife, and seemed more interested in gambling than making a living.

Then again, Ann was the one who received the threat, and he had met her mere moments ago. This couldn't be related to Dash. *Could it?*

Her voice caught his attention again. "For now, we should table our discussion about you. Focus on LubeRoyal instead. We'll need to hold a press conference as soon as we get there. Rather than talk conjecture and supposition, let's discuss our certainties and what we know."

"Impossible. We don't know anything for certain."

"We know that. We know that we don't know anything. That's

something to tell the media. It's important to tell them what we know, what we don't know, and what remains uncertain. That way, we build credibility. They'll learn that we're aware of their information needs."

"I don't know ... If we at least figured out who's behind this, then we could deal with it. Wouldn't a better approach be to secure command and control, gather the facts, resolve the crisis, then talk about it?"

"Certainly not." She chuckled. With a tone laced in sarcasm, she asked, "Where did you learn your battle strategy, Mr. Kassel? Iraq?"

"Some there, yes, but mostly in Afghanistan."

Her face paled and her shoulders dropped. "I'm sorry. I didn't mean..."

"It's okay. I get that those battles are a little different than these." She bit her lower lip. "Thank you for having served. Were you Army?"

"SEALS."

He could feel her gaze intensify, but he didn't take his eyes off the road.

"As in Navy SEALS? The Sea, Air, Land Teams?"

Logan nodded.

"But you're not anymore? Why did you leave it? How did you end up in this line of work?"

No way was he going to talk about his former life or how his men died in that Afghan wasteland. He forced a half smile and met her gaze. "Shouldn't we table that conversation, too?"

She turned red. "Right. Back to the news media." She shook her head once as though trying to secure a new focus. "We must be completely forthright. Let them know we're trying to get answers. This will also buy us some time and establish trust."

Now that he did like. He always appreciated honesty above everything else. He wasn't so sure this plan would go over well with Lube-Royal management, especially Tate, but it didn't hurt to set the wheels in motion. "All right. But before I explain the mixing process we used last night, let me brief you on what it is we do so you can represent us more fully."

"No need. I'm aware of your company, its structure, and its products. We can jump straight to the accident."

He shot her a look of doubt.

Her eyebrows shot up. "Care to test me?"

He grinned. "If it's like your delivery in Bromberg's office, then no, I'll pass. How do you do that?"

"Just a good memory."

"As in photographic memory?"

"Something like that. Pop culture calls it eidetic memory, but the concept is debatable."

"That must intimidate the people in your life." *Particularly the men.*

She half-smiled. "Sometimes. What they don't realize is that photographic memory is unconnected to intelligence levels. It doesn't mean I have command of the knowledge, just that I can memorize it."

"How did you learn this work?"

She studied him a long moment before answering. Logan suspected she wasn't sure how much of herself to reveal. "I was a reporter for several years but became disillusioned with the work. One day I was assigned to cover a company experiencing a crisis due to a disgruntled employee. It was a good company. They'd done a lot of positive things in the community. Helped several non-profit organizations. But the company was unprepared to deal with the media onslaught."

"Sounds like most companies. The unprepared part, I mean." Not the part about helping the community. *Upper management at LubeRoyal, for one, was all about profits.* Just another reason he couldn't wait to get out of there.

"They kept saying all the wrong things. It didn't seem right that one employee's bad behavior should hurt everyone else that worked there. So I stepped across the line. Literally. From one side of the microphone to the other. Rather than watching them fail, I started coaching and coordinating their efforts."

He exhaled a whistle. "That took guts. Let me guess, it cost you your job."

She nodded. "My camera man phoned back to the newsroom. Next thing I knew, my editor called to fire me. I'm not proud of that moment, but it worked out in the end."

"How so?"

"Sam and Webb were there, helping the company with technical response. They liked what I did and talked to me about joining them. We created our own firm."

She stopped and put her hand to her forehead, as if realizing she'd just shared a personal story and wished she could belatedly stuff the words back in. "Speaking of Webb, I should call and have him meet us there."

Logan wondered about the wisdom of her idea. After all, this Webb guy might be part of the problem, despite her high praise of him. In his experience, those kinds of guys were often the ones you had to watch the closest.

"Why him?"

"He's returning from Philly at this moment. He'll drive past Baltimore. He can help with the tech response from the drum storage area. I'll oversee the management and communication."

"What about your team?"

"They're well-trained." Her professional take-charge tone had returned. "They could handle it. But I always prefer Webb or Sam when I can get their assistance. All three partners have trained one another in their specialties. Generally, Sam does management, Webb the technical, and I oversee the communication response with social media, news media, government officials, and customers. So, it will work more smoothly if I can put Webb in the field with your employees."

After disconnecting from her call with Webb, she said, "He's happy to help. Thrives on this stuff, especially the fieldwork."

Ann's mention of Webb working in the field reminded Logan of some bad news. "Collier said our guys stacked too many drums last night. Exceeded our permit. They made a mistake, but I'm certain it wouldn't have caused the explosion. Plus, there are still those bomb casing pieces Collier and our team found to be considered."

Without hesitation, Ann said, "Good to know. I'll tell the media first thing."

Logan's stomach clenched. *Was she that desperate to bring LubeRoyal down?* "Are you kidding?" He hadn't meant his voice to sound snide. "Why would you broadcast our mistakes if it doesn't even come up?"

"You have to tell it all and tell it fast. Even the bad. If the media find out on their own—and they always do—it will be harder on your company. You'll look like you're trying to hide something. You have to stay ahead of the story."

"Jonathan Tate won't like that. He's the—"

"Executive Vice President."

Logan frowned. "He won't agree to that plan. We'll have to figure out a different strategy."

Then again, Logan wondered, what does he care what his uncle thinks anyway? This was Ann's fight, not his. Tate pushed the border line of ethics in the name of profits all the time. In fact, Logan had lost count of the number of lies he'd heard coming from Tate's mouth. Another reason LubeRoyal would get his devotion for only two more years. Then he'd get out of there and back to what he wanted to do— carpentry. That, and the covert consulting he conducted for the SEALS from his cabin.

Sure, Tate would be infuriated, but their agreement would be over. Besides, Tate had been a lousy uncle to Ginny and him.

"Mr. Kassell?" Ann's voice suggested she'd been trying to get his attention.

"Sorry, call me Logan. We're going to have a long day together. You were saying?"

"Just that I'll talk to Tate. I've dealt with his type before. We'll need to set up a command center and a briefing coordination area."

"Make a list. I'll phone it in and get the staff started on it." He had said prayers before that hadn't been answered. Would this one?

She jotted notes while he focused on the traffic, wondering why it felt like LubeRoyal was waiting for them with all the patience of a crouching lion.

And why that van three vehicles back had stayed on their tail since D.C.

He sent up a prayer for fortitude.

CHAPTER TWO

"Then we're in agreement?" Ann canvassed the LubeRoyal representatives seated around the conference table. The VPs from the business development and regional operations shot her dazed looks, while the directors from communications and government affairs simply appeared overwhelmed. Around them, phones rang, workers hurried to hook up computers, frazzled clerks updated status boards, and department heads moved in and out of the crowded conference room.

She spotted Logan in the back talking with the head of the environmental services department. He raised his chin in acknowledgement even as he continued his conversation.

The man may be a bit overbearing—even boorish in ways—but he was impressive. When they had arrived, he'd introduced her to the varied executives then taken immediate command, tossing—and *keeping*—multiple proverbial balls in the air at one time. His staff had done an admirable job of equipping a command center and media briefing room based on the directives he phoned in. It was clear the LubeRoyal employees respected him.

Then again, he may have a centered stillness about him she admired, but he also bore a hum of coiled energy as if he could launch into motion faster than she could blink. No doubt his staff held him in high esteem for that as well.

Perhaps that's why she had panicked when he abruptly maneuvered her from her office in D.C. Sure, she had a flashback of her ex-boyfriend, but Logan was nothing like Aiden, was he? She'd be best to remember her pledge to stay away from men in suits. They were nothing more than wolves in sheep's clothing. Even if this wolf had once been a SEAL.

Besides, this guy acted like *she* was a suspect in LubeRoyal's explosion.

Ann wrestled her gaze from him and snapped back into the moment. "I'll give a summary of what we know and what we're investigating. Then provide an overview of the company. Next, I'll introduce your Director of Public Relations and explain he will be speaking for the company in future briefings. It's important Mr. Tesslar become the face of LubeRoyal, not me. Last, I'll field a few questions from reporters and announce the next briefing for—" She looked at her watch. "—eleven a.m. That should give the representatives from the EPA, OSHA, and local authorities time to arrive and join us."

Like bobble head dolls, the participants at the table nodded in befuddled agreement.

"Great," Ann closed her notebook. "Let's do it." Everyone at the table stood and dispersed, except Tesslar who remained at her side.

"Just a minute, McCarthy," a gruff voice boomed from the right by way of a greeting. Ann gazed up to see Jonathan Tate storm into the room from the command center. His countenance reminded her of a prowling tiger that hadn't eaten in a week, and she was to be dinner. A cold chill swept down her spine.

He was a tall man, late fifties, and his movements were stiff, as if he were either ill-at-ease in his own imposing frame, or perpetually posing for a photograph. As he moved, employees scurried from his path. He gestured a callous motion for Tesslar to make himself scarce. In a challenging voice he addressed Ann. "My staff says you're going to tell the media about our permit violation?"

"That's right."

"We had a death out there, and you want us to admit fault? Have you lost your mind?" His body swelled.

The chatter around her stopped as gazes darted their way.

Ann firmed her shoulders. "Mr. Tate, we won't be admitting fault for the death. Just to the fact that we know we exceeded the permit maximum. I will explain there is no reason to believe one situation led to the other."

"Ms. McCarthy," he said her name with a frosty tone, the way he might say *you idiot*. "We pay a lot of lawyers a lot of money to give us excellent counsel."

"But announcing this—"

He raised a stopping hand. "They say this is legal suicide. Are you telling me they're wrong?" He stared her with such intensity and suspicion, she found it hard to breathe.

She lifted her head higher, aware of the hush in the room. She could feel everyone watching and listening despite awkward attempts not to. "I'm not saying they're wrong. I'm saying they're not the most right in this instance."

He smirked. "What's that supposed to mean?"

"You violated a permit. The media *will* find out. Right now, the crisis is the explosion. That's your story. But if you lie or omit information, then your response will become the story. People will talk about an alleged cover-up longer than they will an explosion."

He brushed a hand down his cheek and across his lips, shook his head as though in doubt. "If you go out there and admit to this violation then it can be used against us in a court of law."

"Yes, it can, Mr. Tate. But it's the truth, isn't it? History has shown most companies recover more quickly from the court of legal opinion than from the court of public opinion. You have a good reputation with the media and with your neighbors and suppliers. Do you want to destroy that now?"

"Of course not," he hissed. "But the notion that this permit has anything to do with the explosion is nonsense. It's perception, not reality."

"But in a crisis, perception is your reality. That's what you have to work with."

Tate scowled, his brows knitting, but he remained quiet as he reflected on what she'd said.

Ann capitalized on his hesitation. "A crisis is a company's defining moment. It can speak volumes about who you are. You can even use this situation to your advantage, to teach the public what it is you do here, and to demonstrate how forthright and honest you are."

Tate's gaze jerked to Logan who was staring at them, despite standing on the opposite side of the room. Ann watched their glares lock. Was there distrust or collusion between these two? She couldn't be certain.

Tate looked back and leaned toward her, his hands fisted, his tone harsh. "Fine. We'll do it your way. But hear this, Ms. McCarthy, Lube-Royal is probably large enough to survive this advice if it is wrong, but you are not. If this backfires on us in any way, I will make sure your company never works again in this industry."

A whisper of dread emanated in Ann's stomach. Her mouth opened, poising the thought, "Are you threatening me?"

Instead, a new voice spoke out. "She's right, Tate." A thin, pony-tailed man in his mid-thirties stepped close, tucked his yellow hardhat under his elbow, and offered his hand to Ann. "Sound advice, Ms. McCarthy. I'm Ford Nichols. OSHA's regional field rep." He turned his attention to Tate. "I just came from the drum storage area. I made a note to check your permits. I would have mentioned the violation at the next briefing. Woulda' looked bad coming from me."

Tate lifted his granite chin at the man's revelation but smoothed his expression before turning to face him. The smile he offered reminded Ann of an actor playing a role on stage. "Ford, nice to see you as always. You know we pay top dollars for excellent counsel like Ms. McCarthy's." He patted Ford on the back. "We want to maintain our reputation for honesty and integrity."

One of Ford's eyebrows shot up, but he let his reaction fall into a lopsided grin. "Yeah, something like that." He turned to Ann, mumbled, "Good job," then headed toward a side table that held coffee and pastries.

Tate grimaced at Ann, as though she were to blame for the awkward exchange he'd just had with the OSHA representative. In a hushed tone, he said, "Are you going to discuss that ridiculous bomb theory, too?"

She shook her head. "That's part of a criminal investigation and can't be discussed yet. Later, the media will understand that necessity. Besides, they want accurate facts. For the scrupulous media, an inaccurate story is worse than no story."

He studied her with a disarming intensity. Between gritted teeth, he said, "Just tread carefully, Ms. McCarthy."

Was he delivering a darker threat?

She pushed her shoulders back, distaste for this man so strong she could practically chew it. His behavior reminded her too much of Sam's grousey attitude lately. No wonder they'd been the two to sign this contract between their companies.

Her mind flitted to Logan's words earlier about seeing her partner Sam with a blonde. Tracy from the coffee shop? If so, why had she looked so uncomfortable about being recognized? Sam had a history of separations with his wife. Separations that he saw as license to date other women. Could he be up to those old tricks again?

She ignored Tate's warning. "If you'll excuse me, we have a briefing to conduct."

Mr. Tesslar stepped in line behind her, following her like a shadow, such that when she stopped by Logan, Tesslar almost bumped into her.

"Webb is corralling the field team?"

"First thing he did. And you're right," Logan offered with a lopsided smile, conciliatory in its delivery. "He seems like a decent guy. Doing a good job at explaining to our crew what information management might need in the command center."

"Perfect. Would you hold onto this for me?" She handed him her cell phone. "I changed the notification settings so you can read any text that comes in. If Webb texts with the drum storage numbers I've asked him to get, then have someone signal me from the back of the room and I'll share that with the media. They love numbers."

"Will do. We'll all be watching." He gestured and she turned to see video equipment had been set up for response teams to watch the briefings.

"Excellent. Can you assign a reliable person to make a list of the questions I'm not able to address? We'll need to provide those answers as soon as possible."

"Consider it done." His tone lightened. "Break a leg."

The briefing went well. More than three dozen reporters, photographers and videographers packed into the room.

For eight minutes, she apprised them on the events in the storage yard and followed the strategy she'd outlined to LubeRoyal's team.

When she offered to take questions, they came at her fast and furious, as though she were extracting buckshot from her skin as quickly as possible. No, she couldn't share the name of the victim. Yes, LubeRoyal would tell them as soon as possible. No, she wouldn't speculate on the cause, and no, there was no reason to believe that anyone living in the vicinity was in danger. She refused to take hypothetical questions, and on any inquiry laced in accusation, she bridged to a point she wanted to make.

She felt good about every part of the briefing but one—that scowling man in a trench coat standing in the shadows in the back of the briefing room.

LOGAN LOOKED around the hushed room. All eyes in the command center focused on the monitor, watching Ann. A nod here, a fist-pump there, a murmur of agreement behind him, told him their collective assessment was the same as his: she was owning it.

Of course, that didn't mean she was innocent in how the crisis started in the first place. He'd heard of firefighters starting the same fires to which they responded. Some people would do anything for glory and money and a chance to prove their worth. He tuned back in as she called on a new person.

The reporter stood. "Rex Blakely. *Chesapeake Times*. Many neighbors object to LubeRoyal's chemicals in their backyards since they don't derive any benefit from them. Wouldn't you agree that's a little unfair?"

Ann gestured to the man. "I'm glad you brought up benefits, Mr. Blakely. We know LubeRoyal isn't a common household name. It might surprise you to learn our products are in things you use every day, most likely in fluids in the vehicles you drive, in the soaps and shampoos you use, and in the medicines, you take. That means fewer emissions and cleaner air. A smoother drive. Healthy hair. Safer patient care. LubeRoyal is always looking for ways to make the best better."

Logan smiled. She was good. He almost—*almost*—felt guilty for harboring doubt. He especially liked what she told Tate about a crisis being a company's defining moment. Perhaps most battles were more similar than different after all. He'd learned in Iraq that an individual most assuredly becomes acquainted with his true self against the storm of adversity. But that was before the incident with Dash and his wife.

He wondered if, despite Ann's uptown lifestyle and city gal persona, she might be able to understand him. It would certainly make their work together more cordial. Especially after the crisis when they finally sat down to develop crisis management plans.

He had watched her hold her own against Tate's bullying. Just before she went into the briefing, Logan had wanted to tell her how he admired her determination to do what she felt was right, but an uneasy feeling in his stomach had made him hesitate.

She was just a suit playing a corporate game. She had a vested interest in her firm's performance today. Besides, her involvement in this accident was still questionable. So, when she'd left for the briefing, he had settled on 'break a leg.'

Lame, for sure. But what did it matter? He'd learned not to trust. *Anyone.* He had been placed in the foster care system when he was thirteen. Twenty-one years ago. Several foster parents had voiced interest in adopting him but never did. His biological mother had repeatedly promised "just six more months" but never collected him. Drugs always won out over him. Once, he'd trusted the wrong man in battle. That had gotten men killed.

No, no more trusting. He'd make sure Ginny learned this prudence, too.

Ann's cell phone buzzed, and he tore his gaze from the monitor to pick it up. A text message appeared, identifying the caller as Aiden Rutherford. He read the message: "A.G., we need to talk. Urgent. Tell no one. Call me."

Tell no one? A message from a man during a crisis, on the same day she finds a threat in her bag and this caller insists she tell no one?

Why did he suddenly feel like he'd been played for a fool?

He looked back at the monitor in time to hear Ann close out the briefing and announce the next one for eleven o'clock.

He stood as she walked back into the conference room to the applause of several employees around him. She blushed and awkwardly accommodated a couple high-fives. Seeing him, she walked over with a smile on her face.

"Well?" she asked. "What'd you think?"

Agitated, he stifled the retort that formed in his mind and reined in his propensity to issue orders in times of duress. Instead, he said, "We need to talk." He gestured to a side room, followed her in, and shut the door.

Ann stared at him with raised eyebrows. "Something wrong?"

He handed her the phone. "You got a text."

Without taking it or breaking eye contact, she said, "Webb?"

"Someone named Aiden Rutherford."

Her body stiffened. Her peach lips formed a straight line as if she were trying to figure things out in her mind instead of drawing forth words to explain.

Finally, she murmured, "That's impossible," more to herself than him.

"Maybe you should read it." He paused then in a more commanding voice said, "Now." He held the phone out again.

For several heartbeats, she continued to look at him then said, "All right." She took the phone, punched in the access code, and called up the message.

He watched her read it. Watched as a shadow covered her face.

"Surely," he said, "you can understand that given our circumstances today, I'm rather curious about this message." That herbal scent of hers filled his senses again as he debated whether he would believe what she said next.

"This ..." Her voice was hoarse. She cleared her throat and started over, meeting his gaze. "This has nothing to do with today's events."

She waved her free hand, discounting the distraction of the text. "This is the past and best left there. We're wasting time—"

"Who is Aiden?"

Her shoulders drooped, and she dropped into a chair. "My ex-boyfriend."

Logan's tone grew hard. "I thought you said there was no one special in your life right now."

She stabbed him with a piercing gaze through narrowed eyes. "There isn't. Did you hear me say ex? As in ex for a long time." Her voice reeked annoyance.

He considered this a moment. "Okay," he offered, but it was laced in a tone he hoped she knew he meant *for now*. "Does he communicate with you a lot?"

"No, not that it's any of your business." She exhaled roughly and rolled her eyes. "He's been in prison. White collar crime. That," she said, steepling her hands on the table, "is another reason he is my ex." Her mouth twitched as if it took great strength not to say more.

He hesitated. Her love life wasn't any of his business, although he wondered why it annoyed him so much. It had nothing to do with the day's events. Still, he couldn't stop asking: "Why did he request you tell no one?"

Her tone grew hard. "Mr. Kassell, I haven't spoken to Aiden since before he went to prison two years ago. I have no idea what he wants or what he intends. Furthermore, I don't care."

"Well I'm afraid you're going to have to care Ann ... or A.G. or whatever your name is." He shifted his stance, startled by the sarcasm in his own voice. In a more controlled tone, he asked, "What does A.G. stand for anyway?"

She firmed her jaw as though defying him to laugh or criticize. "Anna Grace. My full name is Anna Grace McCarthy."

Startled, he stared at her. Was she joking? She may as well have said she was considering joining the circus.

"What?" She pulled her shoulders back and crossed her arms.

He sat. "Anna Grace? It's ... lovely, that's all." *Probably one of the prettiest names I've ever heard.* "But it ... doesn't seem to fit you." The name fit a soft, gentle woman. The kind that enjoyed her femininity and country walks and church socials on Sunday. A self-confidant woman who had her priorities in order, who put family first, not corporate ambition and a materialistic lifestyle.

He jerked back, realizing she might infer an insult tucked in his comment about her name not befitting her. "Why do you use Ann instead of Anna Grace?"

She shrugged. "Anna Grace puts the wrong image in people's heads. It sounds homespun, not professional. No one thinks twice about the name Ann."

Logan rubbed his chin. Of course. This woman was all about image. Hadn't she demonstrated that all morning? Everything she'd said about her work and the advice she'd given, it was all calculated and delivered to leave a certain impression. She'd said it herself: perception is reality.

The perception was she and her company were innocent. But that probably wasn't reality.

Frustrated, he confronted her. "This is your company's third chance this year to make money from clients that don't have their plans developed yet."

She looked startled by the drastic change in conversation, for only a beat. "That's true, but we—"

"In the other two situations, which partner took command?"

"Webb, but—"

Logan scowled. "Webb, the guy you defend the most. The guy we have entrusted with my staff to conduct damage control, to bring this catastrophe to a close."

"What does any of that have to do—"

A knocked sounded. One of the employees from the Information Technology department opened the door. "Sorry, Mr. Kassell, but we need access to this room to set up a few computers."

"Of course." Logan waved the man in. Standing, he took Ann's arm and pulled her to her feet. In a brusque tone, he said, "Come on. We're not finished. We need to go somewhere we can discuss this without being disturbed."

Despite her protestations and efforts to pull away, he steered her out of the room and toward the right. They traversed an empty hall before departing through an exterior door.

"This is ridiculous," she huffed as they stepped into the sunlight. "We're both needed in there. Your staff is still—"

The crack of gunfire sounded and a bullet pinged the metal door about three inches from Ann's head.

Logan grabbed her arm and rushed her sideways in a frenzy as more shots rang out. "This way! To my bike!"

CHAPTER THREE

Ann learned quickly that riding behind Logan Kassell on the back of a Harley at 80 mph provided her with few options to protest. So she did the only things she could: whimper, hold on tight, and pray.

They'd been riding west and north—or was it south and east?—for two hours. She didn't think her adrenaline rush had subsided one bit. She'd swear he took every side road, back road, and dirt road he could find. If her sore backside were any indicator, he had forged a few new roads as well.

During the one brief stop they had made—not a red light, because he sped through all those, but rather to refuel on a quiet stretch of road—she'd barked out as many questions as one could manage in a brief service stop. To his credit, he answered them all:

No, they couldn't have gone back inside the building because he didn't think she'd want to dodge bullet fire while he punched in an access code.

No, he hadn't stolen the bike. It was his, which is why he'd driven the company car that morning.

No, they weren't returning to the corporate office. He was taking them to the "safest place" he knew.

And yes, that was her cell phone he had tossed somewhere between Ellicott City and Frederick because it was too easily traced. Yes, even with the sim card removed.

Yes, legally they needed helmets in Maryland but his was in his office. Besides, if they could secure police attention this way, then so what?

With that last quip for an answer, he had thrust his right leg over the bike and hastened them off to continue the trip.

She held on for dear life, her mind racing. Was the bullet targeted for one of them? If so, which one? Surely not her. She didn't have enemies, certainly none capable of this violence. What had Logan Kassell gotten her into? Who wanted to hurt a company enough to kill for it?

If she wasn't so scared right now, would she be able to chuckle at the picture they presented together on this bike? They both wore suits on a ride that demanded leather jackets. His tie was waving in the air. Her hair had long since blown lose, and her pencil skirt was yanked half way up her thighs. Would passersby get more of a chuckle at her three-inch heels, or his argyle socks?

She groaned at her own ill-timed, crazed thoughts. *Think, Ann! Stop pondering nonsense when your life is in danger.*

Then again, she'd once read how people use humor as a coping mechanism in times of duress.

If she ever got out of this alive, she'd have a lot to laugh about.

Her thoughts were interrupted by the slowing and down-shifting of the bike. She leaned right with him when he pulled into a convenience store.

He parked the bike on the left side of the store and waited for her to get off.

As he put the kick stand in place, he explained, "We're here long enough to get something to eat. That's it. Our escape will be worthless if one of us falls off the bike from hunger."

The place was packed with tall shelves filled with snacks and traveling supplies. Logan paid for sandwiches and soda fountain drinks. Good thing men kept their wallets in their back pockets, because she had no purse, no money, and no ID on her.

They carried their food to a small, plastic table Logan selected, one hidden from the front and both side entrances thanks to the array of shelves.

Before he ate, Logan closed his eyes and bowed his head for a moment before biting into his club sandwich. Surprised, Ann looked down at her own meal and did the same. As she dug into a roast beef, she wondered if his prayer surprised her because he had taken the time to do it, or because he'd taken his gaze momentarily off their surroundings. Up to that point, his eyes had been on constant surveillance of the store.

Neither one of them spoke for the next several minutes. She expected him to share his plans once he collected his thoughts.

Hers meanwhile, were erratic at best. At thirty years old, she wasn't ready to die, and certainly not for the sake of a job. She led a safe, undramatic life, one that consisted of work through the week, roommates in the evenings, and her mother on weekends. In between, she enjoyed music, exercise, and cooking. None of those activities should get her killed. Sure, she had once been an investigative reporter, and she'd rankled a few interviewees through the years when she'd uncovered their dirt. Some ended up in jail or prison. But that was years ago. She couldn't be the target. What in the world was happening?

After a couple minutes of inner turmoil, she grew weary and looked up. "Well?"

His gaze met hers levelly, with intense confusion. "Well what?"

"This." She made a sweeping gesture at the place. "Aren't we going to talk about any of this? Someone shot at us and we haven't discussed who it might be. Why did we leave LubeRoyal? Wouldn't we have been safer there? Are you so certain we were the targets?"

"We'll talk about it when we get where we're going. For now, we need to eat and get moving again." He returned his gaze to their surroundings. Assessing customers that passed them by. Studying the source of each sound he heard. Seeking something at the ends of the shelving units. "Besides, I don't know who shot at us. I assume you'll say you don't either. So there's no answer to that question."

"Yes, but—"

"And regarding your other questions," he stretched his neck as though watching someone pass by on the other side of the shelving, "it didn't strike me as smart to stop in the middle of zinging bullets to discuss our options."

"True, but surely—"

"And yes, my choice to leave may seem hasty, but I didn't think pulling around to the front of the building would be a smart thing to do. Wouldn't you agree?"

"No, I mean yes, I do agree, but I still—"

"By now LubeRoyal knows a shooter was on the grounds. I saw two of our employees running when they heard the shots, too. They dove inside a door further up the alley. They'll alert everyone and the place will be put in lockdown."

"I suppose." She bit her lower lip. "You sure Tate won't try to stop lockdown, too?"

Logan's gaze jerked to her again. "What makes you ask that?"

Ann firmed her posture. "He seemed very determined to ignore common sense response. Like he preferred the company to fail rather than succeed."

Logan hesitated before responding with a crooked smile. "You mean because his opinion differed from yours? No, this shooting was too visible. He'll do the right thing."

She let that go by. "At least tell me where we're going."

"To my cabin in Smithsburg. It's the safest place I know."

"Cabin? Smithsburg?"

He brushed a hand over his head. "Central Maryland. An hour and twenty minutes from Baltimore."

"An hour and twenty minutes?" Ann startled, glancing at her watch. "Why have we spent two hours getting this far?" She pushed the remains of her sandwich away. Her stomach was too anxious to digest anything.

"In case someone is following us."

Ann pressed the lower palms of her hands to her eyes as a narrow ribbon of alarm unfurled in her stomach. *Was someone out there, watching them even now?* It could be anyone and they wouldn't even know. She took a deep breath, hoping the effort would help her recalibrate her thinking. Did she need to reset everything she believed about feeling safe, of trusting blindly in the people she passed by? Their assailant could be anyone. The delivery man who backed his truck up to shops and hauled in soda pop deliveries. The distance runner huffing heavily along the side of the road. The vendor on the street corner who offered a friendly remark each day as she passed by. Is this what life—*her* life—had come to? Her nerves thrashed wildly, like a frantic squirrel, and her heartbeat pulsed in rapid rhythm at the base of her skull.

After a moment she looked up. "That's why you're staring at everything. Everyone. You think—"

He raised a stopping hand at her. "I don't know. You've already received one threat today, and now we've both experienced one. It seems prudent to take this seriously."

Ann thought about that then huffed a short syllable of doubt. "Impossible. Why would anybody want to hurt me? I haven't done anything to anyone. It must be you they're after."

"By placing a threat in *your* purse? Besides, living a life by the rules doesn't prevent you from danger." This time, Logan kept her gaze. "Unlike you, I recognize that anything is possible. People can take offenses at the smallest things. Knowing certain information can put you in danger. Being at the wrong place at the wrong time can sometimes be deadly. Daily interaction with others—each of whom have their own unspoken agendas—can lead to all sorts of misunderstandings. This means anything is possible."

She inhaled a shaky breath. "So, you're saying we need to deal in possibilities."

"No, the stakes may have been raised by big money. I think we need to elevate possibilities to probabilities. Given that we've already dealt with two threats, it's probable there will be more."

Ann felt her eyebrows curve into an anxious arc, but she remained silent, digesting his words.

"Come on. We need to keep moving."

"Let me ..." she began, but her voice was hoarse. "Let me use the restroom quickly."

"Go." He shooed her away. "Make it fast. I'll clean up. When you're done, come straight out the door we went in. I'll have the bike ready to go."

A few minutes later Ann took a deep breath to calm her nerves and left the rest room. She hadn't bothered to look in the mirror because she knew her reflection wouldn't be good and would only delay her.

Back in the main store, she walked by the check-out counter, heading directly to the side door, as Logan had instructed.

"That your boyfriend?" The guy behind the counter asked in bored delivery, looking up from his magazine. "The one driving the bike?"

Ann slowed, a little surprised at the guy's question. *Get a grip. He's an employee, not a threat*. "He's not my—" She stopped. *Why bother to explain?* "Yes, why?"

"Said to tell you he's moved the bike around the building." He pointed to the door opposite the one they came in. "Said he'd meet you out there." He returned his focus to his magazine.

Her heart sped up again. Logan must have seen something suspicious on the other side. She'd better hurry so they could get away quickly. She had already been delayed by another woman ahead of her in line in the restroom.

She exited the building and looked around. No Logan. No bike. To her left sat a large truck blocking her view. She stepped into the parking lot and hurried around the side of the truck. At the far edge of the pavement, back behind a couple dumpsters, sat a wooded lot.

She sensed danger a millisecond before she felt it.

The truck door swung open and a solid presence leaped out, landing behind her. *A man?* A ham-like hand grabbed her around the waist and she screamed as icy dread swirled in her gut. The thug's other hand appeared instantly with a cloth. He quickly and smoothly stuffed it into her mouth as he slammed her head back against his collarbone. Moving his fist to her hair, he twisted it roughly, yanking on her scalp and brutally jerking her head back, sending a shaft of pain down her neck.

Terror skittered down her spine as her feet went out from under her. He dragged her backward, her body held tight against his tall, muscular body. She scrabbled to get her feet solidly beneath her once more. Her heart, already pounding fiercely, accelerated until the thudding of her own pulse drowned out background sounds like the traffic and the store's air conditioning. She felt the footing change from pavement to soil, and watched as, step by step, branches hid them from view.

"Told you to stay out of it. Shoulda' listened." The voice was male, the delivery filled with cold menace. He smelled of tobacco and sweat.

Jagged shards of pain shot like tiny inflamed arrows into her organs, her muscles, her joints. A prayer flooded her mind and heart.

Panic made her lightheaded, but she still had presence of mind to squirm and twist against him all she could. He dragged her backward another two yards, then three, before her writhing caused him to stumble. Down they went together, her hand grazing a rock.

Her self-defense training whooshed through her mind. *Remain calm. Seize the opportunity. Attack vulnerable spots. Make a commotion. Scream!*

Curling her fingers around the coarse rock, she twisted and swung it up in a frenzied arc, smacking him in the head with a thrust that only adrenaline could have accomplished. He cursed and swayed sideways. In another second, she yanked the cloth from her mouth.

For the first time, she realized he wore a ski mask. But she didn't care because she had no plans to stay long enough to memorize his face anyway.

Scrambling to her feet, him grabbing at her ankles, she kicked at him and chucked the rock. It hit in the center of his mask. He cursed again, jerking his hands to the source of the pain.

His momentary surprise gave her the second she needed to break free. Fueled by abject fear, she stumble-ran. But she discovered a terrible truth—her legs didn't want to work right. Weak, dizzy, and rasping for air, she forced herself into motion anyway, her legs shaky and her feet clumsy as she lurched forward.

Please help me! She let loose a scream that would have filled horror film directors with glee.

∞

LOGAN CHECKED his phone when Ann headed to the rest room. A call from Collier, and four from Tate. He ignored the latter, but typed in a text message for Collier: *Can't talk now. U R in charge. CRS's McCarthy w/me. One of us—possible target of shooter. Will call soon.*

First scanning the parking lot, he returned to his bike.

Disengaging the kick stand, he climbed on and started the bike while calculating. They should reach his cabin in forty-five minutes. He wouldn't be comfortable until they'd gotten there, collected his sister Ginny from a neighbor, and secured them all inside his place. If he was the target, Ginny might not be safe either. He'd feel better once he insured access to his weapons, surveillance equipment, and other protective gear. The only weapons he had on him—here, on the open road—were a small pocket knife he kept in his suit jacket, and the Ruger LCP pistol in the motorcycle pouch. He had a concealed permit for the latter, but Maryland had quirky laws about gun ownership and citizens being able to protect themselves. He didn't want to push his luck by carrying it at the ready.

Once at his place, he intended to drill Ann on exactly what secrets lurked in her background she had yet to share. Perhaps on his turf, in his home, with all his things around him and none of her own to buoy her resolve, perhaps then she'd come clean.

When they had talked over their sandwiches, she had seemed to stay stiff with misery and mistrust. He had observed a wave of anxiety creep over her face, heard a drag of doubt in her voice. In her silence, too. At one point, he watched her clamp her lips together, chin trembling. Another time, she'd hugged herself, suppressing a shiver. He'd bet she wasn't even conscious of doing it.

Well good then, she needed to be less trusting if she were, in fact, innocent. In that case, he regretted the directness that had blistered his voice. He hadn't meant to worry her more, just to make her appreciate the gravity of their situation.

Yes, if she were innocent of this whole drama, he could understand the misery. In that case, he wished he could offer her more—a definite answer, a viable solution. But her mistrust irked at him a little. He'd saved her hide from deadly bullets this morning. One had come so close to them he could feel the wind of it passing near his face.

She had done a convincing job of making him think the threat might be on his end. But was that a ruse? Part of a well-honed plan to divert attention from herself and her company? He almost might believe her if that text message hadn't come in when it did. Aiden. Whoever he was.

He didn't know whose name was on those bullets, but if it was his, then she needed to have a long conversation with her partners in crime about how they came a little too close to ending her life as well.

Could she be innocent? Living that transparent, undramatic life she described?

If so, then perhaps she truly was in the dark about this whole mess. Perhaps the threat was on his side, and she had sadly been caught in the middle thanks to her association with CRS and LubeRoyal. Unlike what she claimed, his life had certainly been anything but undramatic up to now. In fact, it was undramatic—even *boring*—that he craved for himself and Ginny.

A review of his life seemed pivotal right now, so he let his mind go back. First, his work with the SEALS. He'd fought in several battles in the Middle East. It was impossible to fight and live in a foreign country—especially ones as deadly and trying on the nerves as were Iraq and Afghanistan—without having disagreements with someone. He had served three tours and seen his share of combat. He'd been involved in close-quarters battle, reconnaissance, long-range desert patrols, personal security, training for foreign allies, and even been shot once and caught up in three separate IED explosions. Death, disillusionment, and discouragement had touched him countless times. And there were always people back in the states who voiced their doubt that, as platoon leader, he had done all he could to save their son or daughter, husband, or wife.

He had a few ex-girlfriends under his belt, too. Each had grown weary, then angry, about his allegiance to returning for more tours of duty. Most recently, Amelia had been a significant part of his life, but he was determined to gain custody of Ginny. Amelia hadn't been receptive to the notion of a ready-made family. Next thing he knew, she had moved to Dallas.

After college and the military, his biological mother had laid a few problems at his feet as well after he'd tracked her down and contacted her. That's when he'd learned he had a half-sister. And that his mother owed a lot of money to angry drug dealers. She'd never paid those debts either; she died from an overdose before they could extract a dime from her. That day, he vowed to act as Ginny's guardian, protecting her, guiding her, and making sure she had every advantage a secure, intact family should provide.

He had no idea who his faceless father was. The man was long gone before he was even born.

Dash. Was he a possibility? Was he back in Logan's life trying to extract justice? Perhaps to place the blame for his miserable life on Logan?

Finally, there was his uncle, Jonathan Tate. Ann had been right when she suggested Tate seemed almost as happy to let the company fail. He'd acted furious with her media briefing plans then changed too quickly after the OSHA rep had voiced his viewpoint. Tate was quite an actor. Logan already knew that. He'd seen Tate pull the wool over many a vendor's and supplier's eyes to get the deals he wanted. As he contemplated, Logan felt a new suspicion lift from the floor of his mind, vexing and irritating him. He needed to have a talk with Tate. *Soon.*

No wonder he trusted no one. His distrust had grown in increments, through accumulation of all these circumstances.

However, he didn't have time to think about that now. He felt like he was strung as tight as a compound bow. He wanted to get home and think, stretch out the kinks, prepare for the unknown. And on the matter of getting home, where was Ann? She should have come out by now.

He revved the bike and inched it forward. May as well make sure she hadn't forgotten and exited out the front. She'd been quite distracted when he told her where to exit the building. She might be standing in front waiting for him all this time.

Once around the corner, no Ann. He dropped his foot to the macadam, preparing to park his bike and go back inside.

A scream sounded from the other side of the building, causing a spike of fear to pierce through his gut.

Ann!

It had to be. A tightness gripped his chest and stole air from his lungs.

He dropped back on the bike and accelerated, racing the machine around the building toward the scream. He didn't know or trust her yet, but she was here at this spot because of him. He'd given her little choice in the matter. Okay, no choice. Besides, he couldn't lose her now. She might be instrumental in solving today's drama.

Regardless, he didn't want her—*anyone*, for that matter—to get hurt.

To his left, he saw Ann racing from the wooded lot behind the convenience store. His heart lurched. Her skirt was torn, the sleeve on her jacket ripped. Scratches covered her cheeks, and she hugged her waist as though she'd been slugged hard and couldn't restore her breathing. She quick-hobbled toward him yelling his name, and for the first time he noticed she wore only one shoe.

He slowed the bike when he reached her, simultaneously pulling the pistol from the bike's attached satchel. "Get on," he yelled, cradling the bike between his legs and aiding her efforts to scramble on behind him. "Are you hurt? How many were there?" he yelled above the noise of the bike.

"One. From that truck." She pointed at it. "Get out of here!"

He understood her fear, her haste to get moving. But the truth was, reaching her, collecting her, and ascertaining the threat had taken less than five seconds. He doubted the bike ever came to a full stop. He didn't need her to tell him to move, that was his intention.

First, he had to ensure a lengthy head start. He snatched the pistol from the satchel and took two shots at the truck, flattening both tires on the driver's side. Then, he twisted the accelerator and they exited the parking lot in a flash.

Once he reached the highest gear and hit a well-surfaced road, he inched an arm behind him and pulled her frame snug into his back, then returned his hand to the handlebar. A risky thing to do, for sure. But of greater concern was the thought she might fall off the bike from fatigue or concussion. He hadn't had a chance to assess her physical state before they'd raced away.

Ten miles down the road, he pulled the bike off onto what looked like little more than a cattle path. He drove until they were well hidden from the Interstate by a rolling hill. The bumping and jarring of the terrain couldn't be good for her, but he had little choice.

When the bike came to a stop, she stumbled off. He caught her arm to keep her from falling.

She pulled away. "I'm fine," she said crossly. Her voice was more tranquil when she spoke again. "Just let me be for a moment."

She took a step, grimacing as though her bare feet weren't used to walking on crude vegetation, then continued, staggering six paces before falling onto a tree trunk. Parking her arms on her knees, she dropped her head between them.

He watched her rasp in deep gulps of air. He wished he could do something for her. "We need to get you to a doctor. Maybe a hospital—"

She looked up and shoved a stopping hand at him. "No! We need to get me to a safe place, that's all. That man was going to kill me," she hissed defiantly. "No more public places. Take me to that safe cabin you talked about. And if you have any more of those pistols at your cabin, I want one, too."

It took her longer than usual to talk because she wheezed, or hiccupped, between every few words. She was either suffering from shock, exhaustion, or bruised ribs. Or all of those. But it was her intensity that startled him most. It was almost manic, an anguish so profound it shook him worse than had her fear. Tight bands constricted around his chest. He hated seeing a woman—*anyone*—so distraught and beleaguered. She seemed on the verge of panic. He'd have to question her later about her gun experience. No way was he putting a fire arm in the hands of a novice.

"Whatever you say," he said gently, pulsing a palm at her.

"And don't patronize me," she growled, casting a sideways stare over her shoulder that startled him. "I'm not hysterical, if that's what you're thinking. The guy hurt my ribs, nothing else. That's why I'm having trouble breathing. I'm not some simpering female or the crying type. I've been a reporter. I've investigated in some rather seedy areas of some rather seedy parts of towns. I've had self-defense training, and I know how to use a gun. My parents always had guns. My dad was a collector, and I grew up shooting sporting clays. Besides, the only reason I was able to run out of the woods was because I fought the guy and escaped—" Her voice hitched.

Probably words of false bravado. Still, she was angry. That was good. Being angry was sometimes an aspect of being hysterical, but now wasn't the time to point that out.

"No problem," Logan said in a flat tone. "I'm not concerned about your state of mind and things you seem to think you can control. My concern is your physical state. I don't want you falling off my bike when we're cruising seventy down the road."

He watched her expression melt, her countenance soften. At least she had the decency to look contrite. "Point taken," she groused.

"We have about a half-hour to go. We've broken several biking laws already. We may as well break another."

"What do you mean?"

"I'll ride in back. Steer from there while holding you in place. You'll have to sit snug toward the front. It'll be a little cramped, but I think we can do it."

"Alright." She started to stand, but staggered. Logan moved close and put an arm around her to steady her.

"One more question ... for now," he offered an apologetic smile. "Did you get a look at the guy?"

"He wore a mask," she said as she progressed slowly—and what looked painfully—toward the bike. "Yes, it was a *he*. I'm sure of that. But I was too busy running for my life to study his height and look for tattoos or skin color."

She tried to lift her leg up over the bike, but failed. Her skirt was ripped. It should have been easier this time. Instead of making a big deal about it, he picked her up and placed her on the bike.

She raised her gaze to him briefly, before dropping her head and looking away again. "You must love this."

Was she kidding? And love what? The fact that for the moment she was dependent on him for survival? That it looked like she had been the target and not him, proving she'd been wrong to suspect him? If she thought he was enjoying this moment of being right, she couldn't be more wrong. If anything, he'd been harboring thoughts of how impressively she'd handled that extreme threat on her life. How she'd kept her wits and gotten away. And her comfort with weapons and experience with clay shooting—intriguing.

Ack, he better stop feeling intrigued by this power-suit woman.

Right now.

"Yeah," he retorted, purposely heaping his voice with sarcasm, "I love this. My idea of a great day."

CHAPTER FOUR

"This view is amazing," Ann mouthed softly, taking in the sweeping mountain panorama, momentarily letting thoughts of explosives and shooters subside. Minutes before, Logan had said the cabin's view stretched out sixty miles to include vistas of Maryland, Pennsylvania, and West Virginia. Far below them in the valley, the terrain was dotted with scattered farms, a small town, meandering roads, and several creeks and bodies of water.

He had excused himself to call LubeRoyal, handing her a pair of binoculars. She used them now to zoom in on a pond on the valley floor, catching sight of ducks as they water-skied to a stop and the tops of trees swaying as a breeze raced through the distant landscape.

A wistfulness snaked through her. Under different circumstances, she would have categorized this as the perfect location for a home. However, after what she'd gone through so far today, a remote and secluded cabin perched on top a mountain no longer struck her as ideal.

The cabin sat at the end of a mile-long private dirt drive composed of steep inclines, several 90-degree turns and as many switchbacks, rising about 1,000 feet above the valley floor.

Far from the maddening crowd. The perfect place to live and work. To sit and soak in the views from the wide veranda fronting the cabin. To secure peace and quiet and conduct research. The kind of work she had long wanted to do: freelance research journalism. From her home, where she could simultaneously take care of her dying mother. Sure, the family farm had views of the mountains, but it wasn't set *on* a mountain ridge like this one.

She had studied journalism at American University in Washington D.C., one of the centers of the news media universe. That's where she met her roommates Rhea Bohannan from Georgia, and Miranda Stanfield from Wyoming. Besides journalism as their major, they shared the same faith, politics, and outlook on life.

Ann had landed a job out of college with the *Baltimore Tribune*. After three years, she'd been ready to leave the profession, having become disillusioned with how editors were forever ordering her to put a biased spin on her stories. Always, their directives accommodated a particular political party, or exploited political correctness. That continued until a stationery manufacturing facility experienced a mishap with one of its pulp mills. She had been disgusted that her fellow journalists were doing their best to paint a poor—and inaccurate—image of the company's safety policies. So, she had put her job in jeopardy and stepped in to help them.

Financially, she hadn't yet been in a place where she could go without a steady paycheck to pursue research journalism, so she joined up with Sam and Webb to form CRS.

Eighteen more months. Then she could sell her portion of CRS, pay off the family farm, and finally parlay her research skills into producing biographies and historical, in-depth research books. Her goal was to research key events in the manner of *The Perfect Storm* and *Seabiscuit.* Even better, she would be present for her mother's last few years, however long they might be. Her mother had many times said she wanted to live out her last days with "views of my mountains." Ann intended to keep that promise.

"Amazing?" Logan stepped to her side and tracked her gaze. He had changed into a Pittsburgh Steelers jersey and jeans. "You'll get no argument from me."

She dropped the binoculars to look at him. The contentment on his face as he stared at the scenery spoke volumes about his feelings for his property.

"I feel closer to heaven when I'm here," he added, a wistful note in his voice. "I will lift up mine eyes unto the mountains, from whence cometh my strength."

Ann studied his profile as he soaked in the view. His close-cropped dark hair epitomized the no-fuss, no-nonsense kind of guy he was. He looked relaxed, a soul at peace in his own domain and unfrazzled by the outside world.

The man was an enigma. He worked in Baltimore but lived on a mountain. Wore suits, but drove a Harley. Commanded a white-collar power job, but she had felt safe when his taut muscles had trapped her against him on the bike. What's more, he had said he—she was certain he distinctly said *he*—had built the cabin. The structure was two-story with four of six rooms finished on the first level. The upstairs was unfinished as well, but would be divided to include two bedrooms and a bath. On the main floor, the three large front rooms—a large kitchen/dining area, a living room, and his sister Ginny's bedroom—sported massive windows, making the mountain views only a glance away. Logan's bedroom and office were in the back of the place. One of the other unfinished rooms already housed exercise equipment.

Logan had said that once the cabin was complete, he would turn Ginny's room into his office and she would move upstairs for more privacy.

The man was methodical, a planner. Even in the face of adversity, he owned himself—his thinking, his outlook, his self-assurance. For a moment, she wondered what it would be like to lean on him just long enough to restore her own strength and conviction. Ugh. She hated how one creep could make her feel so desperate, so helpless. She had let the thug rob her of her tenacity and dignity.

As though oblivious to Ann's thoughts, Logan said, "The treeless ridge behind us backs up to South Mountain State Park. Beyond that is Catoctin Mountain Park. The only other neighbors even close are a buddy of mine and his family. A wife and little boy. They're about a half-mile down the ridge." He pointed east. "I sold them the lot. We have a trail between our two cabins. We help each other when we can.

Ginny plays with Ethan, who's four. Don was a SEAL, too. Now an EMT. I called him after talking to Collier. He's going to collect Ginny for me and check you over when he drops her off."

She felt her face warm. "That's not necessary."

"Perhaps not, but it won't hurt."

She moved to the dining table and sat. "You trust this guy?"

Logan let out a dismissive snort and turned to stare at her, his gaze hard as flint. "I wouldn't work with him, if I didn't."

She blinked. His strong reaction left little room for argument.

For now.

Logan walked to the two-way fireplace that serviced both the dining area and the living room. For the first time, Ann noticed he had started a fire. He bent to gather logs from a black bucket and fed them to the blaze. The dry wood crackled. "Early May can still be cool in the evening. You warm enough? What about thirsty?"

She nodded then realizing he wasn't looking at her, added, "Warm, yes. Tea would be nice. And I'm feeling better, too. Breathing is fine. Pulse is back to normal. There's no need to cause a fuss by having your friend come over."

"No fuss. Don is bringing you clothes and sneakers, too. I think you're about the same size as his wife Meira."

"Clothes? I can't stay here. You must take me to D.C. I'll be safe once I'm in my own apartment."

"You willing to put your roommates in danger, too?"

"What? No, of course not. I ..." She grew silent as it dawned on her he was right.

"Okay, but I still need to call one of them. We keep track of each other. They're in the media business, too. They'll have heard about LubeRoyal. When I don't come home, they'll worry."

"That's not a good idea." He picked up a wrought iron poker and stoked the fire, the embers hissing at the disturbance. "For their own safety, they shouldn't know where we are."

"Not a problem. The three of us long ago established contingency plans. All I need to say is Plan B. They will know not to ask questions and to watch their backs. Besides, they're both still at work. I'll call Rhea. Probably get her cell anyway."

Logan's eyebrows twitched together in puzzlement. "You were certain earlier no one could be after you."

"I was ... *am* certain. It's been years since we established this plan, but they'll remember. All three of us were reporters at one time. We had our share of people being unhappy with our coverage. Miranda and I have long since left the reporter's life. She's now a freelance fashion photojournalist for some rather big magazines. But Rhea is still an active reporter, so we've kept the Plan B option alive. It means to watch your back because someone may be angry at the other of us."

He looked skeptical but fished in his pocket and retrieved his cell phone.

As she received it, she raised an eyebrow in mock indignation that *he* still had a cell phone, but had tossed hers.

"Mine can't be traced." His eyes glinted in amusement.

Yes, he'd understood her look.

As Logan walked to the sink and filled the tea kettle, she called Rhea. The call went to voice mail. Ann left a message saying she was fine and that they should observe Plan B. She would call again when she could.

After clicking off the call, her bravado began to fail. Hearing Rhea's voice message made her long for the evening before when the three of them sat around their kitchen table comparing their weekends. She'd had no idea someone would try to kill her the next day.

Stop it, Ann. She would not fall apart in front of this man. *Don't show weakness.*

She walked to Logan and returned his phone. "Your sister is younger than you?"

"Ginny's my half-sister."

"You share a ..."

"Mother. Our fathers have never been in our lives."

How tragic. Still, he seemed okay with it. His expression had remained neutral when he mentioned their fathers. "Your mom also lives here?"

"She's dead."

She watched him swallow before continuing, his eyes holding a weary mix of sadness and futility.

"Overdose. Ginny doesn't know yet how she died so best if it's not brought up."

"I'm sorry." Ann couldn't imagine how such an upbringing must have impacted him. She had always felt loved by both parents. Instead of returning to the table, she dropped onto a stool at the counter that divided the kitchen from the eating area. "Why doesn't Ginny know?" It was none of her business, but curiosity got the better of her.

"She's only eleven." He lifted the whistling kettle from the stove and poured water into a mug as he spoke. "I'll tell her in a few years, when she can understand it better. We were both in the foster care system. By the time I found out she existed, I was grown and she was already five years old. Right after that, our mother died. Mom had placed me in foster care when I was thirteen. I didn't want that for Ginny. So, I pursued legal action to become her guardian. That won't finalize for two more years." He placed the tea in front of Ann. Fragrant steam rose from its center. The intimacy of the situation, exchanging personal information in his kitchen as they were, made her feel uncomfortable. And confused. Why did his presence both relax and rattle her?

"Long wait. That's unusual." *And so was he.* How many hard-working, good-looking bachelors would put this much time and interest into a younger sister that was still little more than a child? Precious few, she was certain. "Who's her guardian now, a foster parent?"

Something in Logan's jaw ticked, and his lips flatlined. "Jonathan Tate."

Ann froze for a heartbeat then cast him a pointed glare. "Jonathan Tate? As in that bossy, overbearing Executive VP at LubeRoyal?"

"The one and only." He sank onto a stool at the opposite end of the counter. "He is our dead mother's brother. And no, before you ask, there's no love lost between us." He took a deep breath. "I told you all that to tell you this—I'm beginning to think both you and I may be in danger."

"I thought you were certain I was being fraudulent. That the danger was because of me."

"I still do." He raked a hand through his hair. "The danger, I mean. Not the fraudulence."

She forced a smile. "I suppose that's progress. Why so certain now I'm innocent?"

"The way you trembled on my bike."

She cringed. She'd felt secure on the bike. Despite her tenuous state emotionally, she'd registered his arms around her, the size of him, the muscularity of his chest and arms. How embarrassing that he'd had to use them to hold her upright.

Still, more impressive than his physique was his demeanor and his take charge persona at the scene. He had deftly handled the situation, the pistol, the bike, and her. She envied his calmness under pressure.

On the bike, she had wanted to relax into his strength, his serenity. But even as shocked as she had been after that man had grabbed her, she'd known she would regret indulging her desire to lean on him.

Logan continued. "I know few people who could have faked that trembling. Statements, intents, even screams can all be faked, but terror comes from the core and permeates out. Hard to fake that. He leaned back and clasped his hands behind his neck, a sober expression on his face. "What I'm not convinced of, however, is that your past is clean. But that begs the question then as to why the shooter this morning risked hitting me as well. So, for some reason, one of us, or both of us may be targets. If the latter, then we need to consider our connection."

Ann's shoulders sagged. "CRS and LubeRoyal."

"Precisely. Clearly CRS benefits from LubeRoyal's crisis. But I'm beginning to think LubeRoyal might, too. The damage from the explosion will be covered by insurance. As you told Tate, sometimes a company can benefit, even profit, from a crisis."

An unease shifted in her gut. "You're saying someone from one of our companies may be behind these attacks."

Logan nodded. "Or they hired someone to carry them out."

Ann tried to wrap her mind around it. Tried to think of another answer. There weren't any. She may as well come clean and establish common ground with him. "I'm beginning to agree with you."

He shot her an expectant look, and she shared details of the biker that had crashed into her outside her office building, his threat, and how the thug at the convenience store had referred to it. She told him about the man in the trench coat in the back of the briefing room. "So yes, it might be someone, somehow, affiliated with one of our companies."

"One perhaps. Or two, or more individuals working together. Collier said the shooter hasn't been found, so the facility remains on lock down. The media can't leave, so LubeRoyal went ahead with the second briefing. Tesslar apparently did a good job, and is following up on unanswered questions." He hesitated, intensifying his gaze. "You did good. You set the company up to stay ahead of this crisis. It's theirs to win or fail now. Must be a good feeling."

Was the compliment genuine, or was it a diversionary tactic? Designed to get her mind off the guy who grabbed her?

Regardless, she welcomed the feedback. At least that part of the day had gone well. She was glad he was pleased.

Why did she care what he thought?

She nodded. "It is a good feeling. A business doesn't have to be a non-profit to do good things for people. Employees put their hopes and dreams into a business. They invest their time in it. Put their savings back into it. Rely on it to help them house and feed their families. The money they earn often ends up as donations to charities. The people who think all big business is bad are wrong. Honestly, I wasn't helping LubeRoyal the corporation as much as I was trying to help its employees."

He cocked his head and studied her as if she had grown a second nose. *Was he analyzing her? Gauging her sincerity?* After a moment, he shook his head, stood, and returned to poke at the fire. "Course, Tate's furious we both disappeared. Webb is still there, and apparently, Sam Bromberg is on his way. I asked Collier to let them know you are safe and in an undisclosed location. "Now," he said, turning to look at her, "that brings us full circle. Back to you."

"Me? What about me?"

"I still think the connection may be our two companies. First though, I need to hear more about this Aiden guy."

Logan watched the color drain from Ann's face.

She let out a sputtering, exasperated sound. "Aiden? I already told you I haven't seen or spoken to him in years."

"You said he spent time in prison. You have a history of dating bad boys?" His tone was patronizing and rude, prompting regret to snake through his core.

Her shoulders stiffened, and her head inched higher. "Of course not. Aiden is ... *was* a CPA and tax accountant. Graduated top of his class from Princeton. Comes from an impressive family. He wasn't a *bad boy* when we dated." She hesitated, her mouth twitching as though she had something discomforting to add and had no choice but to share it. Her gaze dropped. "Not at first, anyway."

Good, she was opening up. Logan pressed his advantage. "What's that supposed to mean?"

"Not that it's any of your business ... or even relevant to our discussion, for that matter, but he changed while we were dating."

"How so?"

"At first, he got fidgety. Restless. Couldn't sit still or relax. Always distracted." She leaned back. "Then, it seemed like he was angry all the time. Paranoia set in. He began to dislike and distrust everyone."

Logan's gaze held hers steady. "All signs he'd gotten involved in something nefarious or something over his head."

Ann opened her mouth, but nothing came out. She looked startled at his quick—and apparently accurate—assessment. He suspected she would like to refute it and hated that he identified it so quickly when she had not seen it herself.

"Did he ever hurt you?" He clinched his jaw waiting for the answer.

She grimaced, dropping her gaze to her cup. "You mean physically? Yes, once." She hesitated then said in a hoarse voice. "It was the first and last time."

He said nothing but felt his hands fist. Any louse that would hit a woman was highly suspect in his book. The haunted look in Ann's brown eyes tore at him. He hated making her dredge up what must be a painful memory, but it had to be done. This was work. Life or death work. Emotional concern would only weaken his objectivity.

She continued. "About a year after I ended it, I read in the paper he was convicted of a while-collar scheme and sent to prison."

"Why would he text you saying he urgently needed to see you? Today of all days. And in particular, why you should tell no one?"

She sighed, and he detected annoyance. "I already told you I don't know."

"Would you have called him if the text had come in under different circumstances?"

"I don't know." She emphasized each word, lacing them with indignation. "He was a constant critic of me and my choices, but I've always been taught to forgive seventy times seven, so yes, I might have. You may think me weak for that, Logan, but I'm so indifferent to him that calling or not calling is a non-issue with me. I owe that to Webb and his wife. They helped me see he was wrong for me. Even before he changed. That I wasn't confined to him by choice or love or circumstances, but rather my own psychology." She took another sip of tea before continuing. "I like to think that if I can help someone, anyone, I would. It's what the Bible teaches us to do. But this conversation is moot, isn't it? You threw away my phone, and I don't know his new number."

Logan looked away, not wanting her to read him. He had noted Aiden's number. But now wasn't the time to admit it.

He was stymied by her willingness to forgive. And with her detachment to Aiden. The ability to be indifferent generally suggested significant growth. A generous heart. *If she were telling the truth.*

He stood and paced. "Any chance you know details about what put him in prison? It had to involve money. Thoughts on where he might have hidden it? Anything about the accounts? Can you think of any reason he might find you instrumental in helping him now?"

"No, no, no, and no." Her tone carried a finality to it. She lowered her chin determinedly. "Now, let's talk about you."

The tables had turned. He would have to indulge her questions as well. He stopped and leaned back against the stove, crossing his arms and his ankles. "What about me?"

"You're what? Early thirties?"

"Thirty-four. What's that got to do—"

"Thirty-four. Four years older than me. Four more years to have made friends and enemies. Four more years than I have had on the dating scene. Any angry women in your wake? Perhaps co-workers that you had to discipline or fire? What about men and women you commanded that didn't agree with you? Any disgruntled former colleagues that prompted you to hide yourself on this remote mountain?"

He took his time answering her, picking a couple pieces of fake lint off his shirt to avoid her gaze. Finally, seeing no recourse, he raised his hands. *Fair was fair.* "All right, as long as we're coming clean ... that is what you're doing, isn't it? Coming clean?"

"Of course."

"Fine then." She already knew about his upbringing, so he may as well tell her the rest of his more discouraging history. "I witnessed one platoon mate forcefully shove his wife into a wall. Unlike you, she stayed with the guy, and it wasn't his last time. In the end, for interfering and helping her, it was me that was labeled with PTSD. My esteemed uncle," he said sarcastically, "Jonathan Tate, saw that as his opportunity to blackmail me into serving as his puppet at LubeRoyal for eight years. He said he'd seen me acting violently on several occasions. All lies, of course. I have two years to go before I present a document signed by him stating he was wrong. Then, I'm free of him. After that, I become Ginny's legal guardian, and I can leave LubeRoyal."

Ann looked startled, uncertain what to say. "He sounds very ..." she shot him an apologetic look before finishing, "manipulative."

Logan nodded. "He has nothing else in his life. No kids. Two divorces under his belt."

"How do you know he'll sign over custody?"

"He already has. But cleverly, he dated the document for eight years in the future. That's two years away." He unfolded his arms and placed his palms at his side on the stove front, his back still against it. "The problem is that it's becoming increasingly hard to juggle tolerating his shenanigans with what I feel is right. When I agreed to this whole arrangement, I thought I would be left alone to develop corporate wide physical and IT security, and that it would take my entire tenure. Turns out, the team I selected was too efficient. We developed and implemented a functional program a year before I thought it possible. That, then, has pitted me with Tate more and more lately, working on other projects at his whim. We've butted heads more times than I can count." He shrugged a shoulder. "I confess to having been annoyed when Tate signed a contract with CRS without my input. But I also was glad to take our program to the next level by adding global crisis management response because—"

"… it would keep you busy on our combined project, thereby having to spend less time with Tate."

"Exactly."

"So you're concerned what Tate may ask next of you. Concerned your determination to do what's right might clash with his desires, his ambition. And if he gets mad, he will stop your access to Ginny?"

"That about sums it up. In my favor is the fact that Ginny will be thirteen in two years. By that age, the courts often ask teenagers who they want to live with. I'm sure she'll say me. I've scheduled my hours around her as best I can. I stay in a room at a boarding house near LubeRoyal Monday through Wednesday nights. I work four ten-to-twelve-hour days. Then, I'm back here Thursday night, for three days. She stays with her best friend Angela's family Monday, Tuesday, and Wednesday nights. She's never with Tate and is mostly with me. That time together, combined with character witnesses I have, may be enough to undo any damage Tate tries to inflict. For Ginny's sake, I don't want it to come to that."

A clanging sound cut through the silence in the house. Ann sputtered a small syllable of surprise and jerked to look around, spilling her tea on the counter. "What was that?"

Logan was in motion before she finished her question. Stepping to an upper cabinet beside the refrigerator, he pulled the door open, reached in, and clicked off the alarm. Above the switch, a monitor showed a vehicle approaching several hundred feet down the lane. An old, green Bronco.

"That's Don's car." He checked his watch. "Right on schedule."

"You have a monitor in your—"

He lifted his hand, silencing her.

The Bronco approached, its tires cutting through the gravel. A horn sounded. One long beep then two short ones.

"That's the signal," Logan said as he moved to the door, undid the deadbolt, and opened it wide. "Ginger snap!" he yelled to his sister.

Within seconds, Ginny raced from the car, crashed into his torso, and wrapped her arms around him. With a giggle, she said, "I told you not to call me that in front of people."

"People?" Don asked, lifting bags from the backseat. "Is that what I am now, *people*? When you greeted me ten minutes ago, I was Uncle Don, the best uncle in the world."

Ginny rolled her eyes. "You know what I mean. Besides, you're not really my uncle anyway." She turned her blue eyes back to Logan and that quickly, forgot the clarifier she'd just issued. "Uncle Don said plans have changed. I didn't think I'd see you until Thursday night. What'd you do this time, big brother?"

Logan draped his arm on her shoulders and led her into the house, Don following. "What do you mean this time?"

"Sometimes when you get involved in another mission with your former SEAL mates, you get fussy about things around here. All you can think about is the mission. You usually send me off to Angela's for safekeeping. How long am I going to be with her family this time?"

Logan cringed at what her words implied. If she felt like she was being juggled around, that wasn't good. He would have to think about that one long and hard. *Later.* For now, he wanted her here where he could protect her. "You're not, kiddo. You're staying here, but you may be out of school a day or two. I don't have enough intel to make that decision yet."

Ginny rolled her eyes and grinned. With sarcasm edging her voice, she said, "If I must. But you remember the sacrifice, big brother."

The three of them arrived in the kitchen. Logan gestured a hand at each person, making introductions. "Ginny. Don Amherst. Anna Grace McCarthy."

When he mentioned her birth name, Ann shot him a scowl but recovered quickly to extend a greeting to the others.

Logan looked at Ginny. "Anna Grace is someone from work. We're tackling a project together. So, she'll be with us tonight, too."

Ginny turned to Ann. "That's code for *hush-hush work so don't ask about it.*"

"Very funny, little sister. Here's a code word for you—precocious."

Ginny parked her hand on her hips dramatically. "That's not code. I know what it means. And I'm proud to own it." She looked back at Ann. "Do you play chess? Logan is teaching me, but I've only beaten him once."

Ann smiled. "I do. We'll have to play a game."

"Ginny," Logan said, "that will have to wait. Anna Grace was injured today in a little mishap, so Don is going to check her over."

Ginny shrugged. "Okay. I'm going to go read my email." She headed toward the living room.

"But you know the drill." Logan called after her. "Not a word to anyone—"

"Yeah, yeah, yeah, big brother. I know."

Don handed Ann a brown shopping bag. "Meira put some clothes and sneakers in she claims are versatile. Whatever that's supposed to mean. Why don't you sit, and I'll do a quick exam."

"I told Logan this isn't necessary. I'm fine."

"You're probably right," Don said, lifting a medical bag to show her, "but I'm here and I'm equipped. Why not indulge me? You'll be giving me a chance to one up this guy," he said, gesturing at Logan. "This way, he'll owe me. I don't get many of those chances."

She sighed, removed her ripped suit jacket, and dropped onto a bar stool.

Don was done examining her in less than ten minutes. "Your pulse and other vital signs seem to be fine. Blood pressure is good. No signs of concussion, and all bones seem to be intact. Just take it easy tonight and see how you feel in the morning."

Ann stood. "This wasn't necessary, but thank you all the same." She reached for the bag of clothes and held them up. "Now this, this *is* necessary." She pointed at her bare feet. "Please thank Meira for me. I'll go see if anything fits." She shot Logan an inquisitive look.

"Through the living room and into the hallway. First door on your right."

"Any updates?" Don asked after she left.

Logan filled him in on what little he knew.

Don frowned. "You have no leads on who might be behind this?"

Logan shook his head before Don finished the question. "Nothing more than what I told you."

"Well, as far as unexpected company goes," Don grinned, "she's at least easy on the eyes, pal."

Logan gave a 'whatever' gesture and turned away. "I hadn't noticed."

"Okay, I'll let that one go for now." Don chuckled under his breath. "So why aren't you getting the police involved? The fake bomb, the gunshots, the goon at the convenience store ... sounds like she is the target. Why not let them handle it? And why bring her here? This is mission central for our ops work. We don't need more people coming here and becoming familiar with the place."

"I know. It's just that I'm not convinced this is all about her."

"If not her, then you mean you?"

"Maybe. I find it odd—"

A chime came from his cell phone. Logan picked it up and read the number. D.C. area code. With a thought, he answered.

A minute later he clicked off the call, making a mental note to swap out his phone as soon as this situation was resolved. He didn't need people tracking him to this place. This caller had known his number because Ann used his cell phone earlier.

Logan briefed Don on the discussion.

Don nodded his understanding. "I'll get in touch with Barrett. Get him on it."

Logan frowned. "I don't want to draw unwanted attention to my home, but we can't afford to spread ourselves too thin. So, here is where we'll have to entice our target." Logan looked up as Ann walked into the room wearing rolled-up jeans, a floppy t-shirt and sneakers.

"What target?" Her gaze leaped from man to man. "What's going on?"

Logan took a deep breath, bracing himself to deliver concerning news. "Your roommate Rhea called. She was in a hurry so she talked to me. Your mother called her when she couldn't reach you. She said your mom phoned the police twice today, convinced someone tried to get into her house. The police couldn't find anything, but she thinks they're still on the property." He watched Ann grip the counter edge with a hand as he continued, "This is too coincidental for my comfort. We need to get her out of there. *Now*."

CHAPTER FIVE

A nn gasped as his meaning blossomed, her pulse shooting to staccato rhythm. "What! That's crazy. Who would want to hurt my mom?" In a quivery voice, she continued. "You think whoever is after me ... us ... you think they're now after my mother?"

"We have to entertain any—"

"I've got to go to her." Ann swirled, robotically searching for her purse and keys. Her situation hit her. "Do you have a car I can use?"

Don cut in, looking at Logan. "You two talk. I'll call Barrett from your office." He turned to Ann. "Would you write down your mother's address?"

"What? Why?"

Logan spoke. "Don's going to call a friend to retrieve her. Bring her here."

"No." Ann jerked her head back and forth fiercely. "A *friend*? You're sending a friend into a potentially volatile situation? A total stranger to my mother, by the way, to pick her up and remove her from her house?"

"His name's Lyle Barrett, although everyone calls him Barrett," Logan said. "He's a platoon mate of ours. A former SEAL. Works with us on various projects. Lives in Fairmont, West Virginia. He can probably get to your mom's house quicker than we can. Rhea said your mother lives near Morgantown?"

Ann blinked away his comment, trying to process what he was telling her. Her mother must be terrified. She felt tears welling in her eyes. She turned and walked to the front window, needing a moment to gain her composure. The view that had appeared so enticing and peaceful earlier now appeared bleak and cold as the setting sun darkened the mountains and lengthened shadows.

Ann tried to collect her wits. She would not let them see her break down. Just before she had returned to the kitchen, she wondered if the day could get any worse. That quickly, she learned it had. She closed her eyes. *Please be with my mother. Keep her safe. Comfort her. She's been through so much already.*

"Ann? Time is of the essence." Logan's voice cut through her senses. His tone was laced with determination.

"Y-Yes, all right. Let me write down that address."

Don handed her a pen and tablet he had pulled from his jacket pocket. When Ann was done, he left the room.

She hugged herself, suppressing a shiver. "I need to call Mom. Give her a heads-up. I don't want her getting scared by this Barrett person."

"Or calling the cops on him," Logan added. "That can wait a couple minutes. Let's give Don a chance to set the wheels in motion then you can talk to her. Tell her to pack for a week's stay."

"A week? But why—"

He raised a stopping hand. "Just a precaution. Best to have any prescriptions and toiletries she might need in case this drags on."

She nodded, dropping her gaze to the ill-fitting clothes she wore. "I'll have her pack some of the clothes I keep at her place, too."

"Good idea." He grinned and it made her relax. *A bit.*

"She won't want to come." Ann folded into a chair at the dining table. "She's rather fragile right now and likes being home."

Logan's head tilted, his eyes taking on a warmth that surprised her. "You mentioned earlier something about lymphoma?"

He remembered that? Ann nodded, swallowing away a lump in her throat. "She's dying from it. Slowly."

"I'm sorry." His gaze filled with compassion, and she looked away from it.

"Not long after Dad died, Mom was diagnosed with Sjogrens' Syndrome. It's an autoimmune disease in which the white blood cells attack the adrenal glands. She had developed chronic dry eye and dry mouth while in Zimbabwe, but assumed it was due to the different food and climate."

Logan folded onto a chair perpendicular to her. "Once back in the states, she was diagnosed?"

Ann nodded. "Sjogrens patients are at increased risk of developing lymphoma."

"And that's what happened because she didn't know to look for the signs?"

"We learned too late. She underwent chemotherapy and stem cell transplant, but hers has been particularly aggressive. It spread to other organs. Stage four." Ann slouched, placing her elbows on the table for support. "The five-year survival rate for stage four lymphoma is about sixty-five percent."

"The odds are in her favor, and there are medical breakthroughs every day. Don't worry. She'll be here soon." He sounded certain.

"She gets tired easily. This drama won't help."

"No, but she can relax here." He looked toward where Ginny had exited. "Unfortunately, she probably wants to be in her own environment. Maybe not want to be around Ginny. She's a terrific kid, but all kids can be exhausting." He brushed a hand down his cheek and across his lips. "For that matter, I don't know how Ginny will adapt either. She's used to it being the two of us."

"I guess we'll find out soon."

"We'll park your mom in front of those windows, and she can soak in the view. That should make her happy, right?"

Ann forced a smile. "Maybe. But I must warn you, nothing makes her as happy as the scenery from our farm. She has said many times she wants to live out her last days with views of her mountains."

"I can understand that," he said. He cocked his head and leaned in, forearms on his knees. "Let's table these concerns until she gets here. For now, we need to figure out who's behind these threats today. We're caught in a tug of war, and we don't even know who's on the other side of the rope. The sooner we know that, the sooner we can get your mom back to her own home."

She scowled and razed him with a stare. "I suppose you want to discuss Aiden again."

"I'm guessing he's been to your West Virginia farm?"

"Of course. Many times." She steepled her fingers on the table. "Look, you're right that I don't know what he's like now after two years in prison. But any connection between him and what happened today makes no sense. There's no way for him to profit from our companies succeeding or failing."

A fractious silence fell. For a few heartbeats, there was no sound but the fire. Logan looked like he wanted to refute her logic but could not.

"Besides," Ann continued. "How could he know about the contract between our companies? Aiden is ... *was* a tax attorney at an accounting firm. CRS has never used his firm. I'm guessing LubeRoyal uses in house accountants?"

Logan nodded.

"Aiden couldn't know the terms of the agreement," she said. "I can't attest to any influence Sam may have had in the negotiations or in signing that contract because I wasn't there. Webb either. It surprised us both. But then, Sam has a history of keeping things from us." She paused. "Like his relationships with women."

"I thought you said he's married."

"He is. But they separate a lot. He always seems to find someone in between." A pang of remorse shot through her. *What kind of person would Logan think she was to get involved professionally with a man like Sam? Should she explain her ignorance of his behavior when they launched their firm? More important, why was she suddenly concerned what he thought?*

She drew a ragged breath and continued. "Webb and I have talked about it. Our contracts prevent us from making changes for now. We both have eighteen months before we can cash out." She groaned. "Sorry, I probably shouldn't have told you that. The company will still honor its contracts, regardless of who they get to replace me. Besides, we have eighteen months. We can develop plans for LubeRoyal, even test them, in that time." *Better get off that topic quickly before he gets concerned about her company's viability.* "Anyway, neither Webb nor I were there when this deal between our companies was struck, so I don't think Aiden—"

Logan jerked his shoulders back and cocked his head. "Wait a second. Are you saying that you or Webb usually are present when contracts are signed?"

Ann nodded. "Always. One of us. The two-heads-are-better-than-one theory. At the very least, during the negotiations. That's when we learn the full scope of work and figure out the terms."

Logan stood and paced again, his mood seeming to have shifted in the blink of an eye. She was startled at the change her comment wrought in his expression.

Finally, he spoke. "That's interesting because I'm usually involved also in any contracts that impact security. This deal took me by surprise, too."

Her pulse thumped in her ears. "You think this is the connection, don't you?"

"It's possible."

Ann recalled their earlier conversation about possibilities verses probabilities and, despite her agitation, forced a sheepish grin. "Not probable?"

The corners of Logan's lips inched up. "Not yet, but it's moving in that direction."

"You already pointed out that CRS stands to make quite a profit if LubeRoyal has a crisis before management plans are established. What about LubeRoyal? How could Tate possibly benefit personally if the company suffers?"

Logan hesitated. "I haven't figured that out yet, although I could make an educated guess." He looked toward his office. "Don should be done talking to Barrett by now. Why don't you use the office to call your mom?"

As she pushed back from the table, Ginny walked into the room. "What's for supper?"

"Then," Logan shot Ginny a look, "I'll figure out what there is to eat around here. It's going to be a late night."

"I'll cook," Ann offered as she stood and stretched.

Logan squinted in disbelief.

She shrugged. "It's not 'women's work' to me. I love to cook. It's my therapy. I consider myself a creatrix in the kitchen."

"May I help?" Ginny asked. "No one—" She shot a chastising look at Logan. "—will take the time to teach me."

Ann smiled. "Of course. I would love your help." *The more distractions the better to take my mind off Mama.*

LOGAN LEFT HIS OFFICE, heading for the kitchen where—if the aroma was any indication—Anna Grace and Ginny were making spaghetti and garlic bread. It had been an hour since they had set the wheels in motion for Barrett to retrieve Anna Grace's mother.

No, *Ann's* mother.

As though his feet mirrored his mind, he hesitated. He turned to the living room window, needing a moment to process his thinking. He had thought of her just now as Anna Grace. Why? She'd been annoyed when he had introduced her in that manner. Was it his imagination or was she beginning to fit the name? When did that happen? He shook his head at his musings. He was feeling sympathetic toward her after the day she had. *That's all it was.*

Logan stared into the darkness. The light of the distant moon grazed the peaks of the mountain ranges and fell into the valley where it glittered on several ponds and streams. *God, you made these mountains and this beauty. There isn't anything you can't do. Please keep Mrs. McCarthy and Barrett in your care.*

He turned and moved toward the kitchen. At Ginny's voice, he stopped at the doorway to watch. He could see them, but they weren't aware of his presence.

"I don't mind missing school, of course," Ginny said as she peeled a carrot. "But I'll miss my friends. And I don't want to fall behind on my geography project. It's about Egypt and the pyramids."

Ann pulled a pan of garlic bread from the oven and turned off the broiler. "I loved studying Egyptology in school. You shouldn't have much trouble finding credible sources on the Internet."

Ginny put down the peeler and picked up a paring knife. "Am I doing this right?"

Ann glanced over. "Perfect. Be sure to slice away from your fingers."

Ginny tilted her head in thought. "The problem is, I have to use certain sources from the Maryland library system. But I can't figure out how to access it." She tossed the carrot slices into a salad bowl, watching them land on the lettuce.

"I can help you with that."

Ginny beamed and turned to her. "Would you, Anna Grace? That would be awesome."

"Of course. That's my kind of fun. Give me something to research and I'm all over it. I don't stop until I've exhausted everything." She pulled a cucumber from the refrigerator. "Since you're so good at peeling and chopping, why don't you attack this cucumber next and add it to the salad? The bread and spaghetti are done. Just another minute for the sauce."

"Do you do that with your work? Research, I mean?"

"No." Ann knitted her brows. "But one day I hope to. It's much more rewarding to me than what I'm doing now."

Logan remembered Ann saying she could cash out of her company in eighteen months. It sounded like she already knew what she planned to do after that. The quiet life of a researcher sure sounded more like an Anna Grace than what she was doing now.

He rolled his eyes at himself. He barely knew this woman. How could he draw assumptions like that? He better make a concerted effort to refer to her as 'Ann'.

Ginny started peeling the cucumber. "I don't think Logan is very happy with his work either. He's grumpy on Thursday nights. But by the weekend, he seems happy again. He's either doing a carpentry job for someone or working with what he calls his merry band of brothers."

Time to interrupt this discussion before it goes any further. Still, he was impressed with how well Ann and Ginny were getting along. And at how devoted Ann was to her mother. Despite holding a pleasant conversation with Ginny as they cooked, she seemed distracted and wore the stress on her face. No doubt she was worried about her mother and was trying to cover it up.

"Something smells terrific," he said as he entered the kitchen.

"Logan!" Ginny said. "I know how to make garlic bread crispy now. And how to keep spaghetti from sticking together."

He pouted in a jesting manner. "Something tells me there's a lot of spaghetti suppers in our future."

"Anna Grace promised to show me how to make pot roast sometime."

Ann looked at Logan. "I hope you're right that we shouldn't have waited for Barrett to arrive. I know my mom would not want to eat this late, but I'm not sure about him."

"Barrett's a grizzly of a guy. Trust me when I say he'll swing through a drive-through and eat something on the way."

An hour later, with supper and clean-up behind them, they watched a shaft of light cut through the hillside and spill on the long incline to the cabin. Barrett had called moments before saying they were almost there. Shortly, the alarm chimed, followed by a horn sounding. One long, two short.

Following introductions, Ann hugged her mother for a second time. "I was so worried about you, Mama. I'm sorry we had to send Mr. Barrett to get you like this."

"Anna Grace," Mrs. McCarthy admonished shaking her gray-haired head, "Don't be silly. Lyle and I got along swimmingly."

"Lyle?" Ann cast her mother a curious look.

Six-foot-four Barrett beamed and looked at Logan. "Did you know Delores taught finance at West Virginia University?"

"Delores?" Ann looked from Barrett to her mother, her brows inching higher.

Unfazed, Barrett continued. "She explained the stock market to me in a way that finally makes sense. She knows a lot about essential oils, too. She gave me ... what was that stuff again?"

"A mixture of eucalyptus and peppermint," Mrs. McCarthy said.

"Yeah, that's it. A little dab on my temples and boom." He clicked his fingers. "Headache was gone in minutes."

Ann gazed at Logan and he shrugged.

Mrs. McCarthy looked around, her movements gentle, unhurried as though she were too frail to do more. "Your home is beautiful, Mr. Kassel. Lyle said you built it yourself?"

"Logan, please. And yes, I did. I hope you'll be comfortable here."

Mrs. McCarthy waved it off. "I'll be fine." She looked at Ginny. "You are a very pretty young lady. How lucky you are to be able to grow up on a mountain. I bet your friends don't have a place like this, do they?"

Ginny cocked her head in thought. "No, Ma'am, they don't. Wait until you see the view in the morning."

"I look forward to it."

Logan's cell phone rang and he read the caller ID. *Collier.* Every muscle fiber tensed. They'd been in contact all day, but this call was coming too late at night to be a mere update. He excused himself to take the call in the next room.

When he returned, he heard Ann saying, "No, Don went home. Earlier, Logan explained the sleeping arrangements to me. Mama, you and I will sleep in his room. He'll use the fold-out couch in the living room. And Barrett, apparently, there's a bunk bed in the unfinished room upstairs you're already familiar with?"

Ginny looked at Mrs. McCarthy and said, "Would you like to see the rest of the house?"

"I'd like that very much. I especially want to see your room. I bet it's pink or purple."

Ginny's eyes widened. "How did you know?"

"Let me tell you about Anna Grace's room when she was your age," she said, following Ginny from the room.

Logan watched them leave before stepping closer to Ann and Barrett. "There's been another development."

Ann's shoulders dropped. She cast him a wary look. "What now?"

"That call was from Collier." He looked at Barrett and clarified for him, "At LubeRoyal." His gaze returned to Ann, and he reached out to place both hands on her upper arms, drawing her eye to eye. "There were more shots after we left. I'm sorry Ann, but Webb has been seriously injured."

She closed her eyes against the blow and a strangled sob escaped her lips. "Webb?" she whispered at last. "Where? How?"

"At LubeRoyal. The drum area. He was hit in the chest."

"The chest! But—" Her voice broke, and she pulled her arms free to place her hands over her mouth.

Logan's heart sank at the sight of her distress. He wished he had better information to share, but he didn't, so he plunged ahead. "He's in critical condition. They've life-flighted him to Johns Hopkins Hospital. For now, it's touch and go."

CHAPTER SIX

By 2:15 p.m. the next day, Ann pulled Webb's wife Tia into an embrace. "You heard the doctor. He's strong. Tough. He made it through surgery." She took a deep breath, trying to prevent it from revealing the anxiety she felt. How could she be strong for this woman when she herself felt like she might break down at any moment?

Webb had always been there for her. Helped her through the whole Aiden ordeal then got her involved in church again. He had been the one who reminded her God was in control and she should let Him do what He does best. It was then she determined to stop moving forward with notions of faith in her *own* abilities, and instead to trust in something bigger than herself.

Tia sniffled and dabbed a wadded hankie at her eyes. "I know. If he makes it through the next twelve hours—"

"He will," Ann declared, hoping she sounded convincing. "He has to." The doctor had described Webb's status as "cautiously hopeful." She glanced back at Webb, lying on the bed, at least four tubes and gadgets attached to him. The steady sound of the heart monitor had begun to thrum in her brain.

He was a muscular, solidly built man who exercised regularly and ran 10Ks. Seeing him like this—helpless and dependent on machines—was almost a surreal experience.

"Thank you," Tia said. "You're always such a good friend to us." She dropped her gaze to her hankie. It was twisted around several of her fingers. "Why would someone want to do this? Webb is such a good man. He wouldn't hurt a fly." She hesitated. "I'm sorry. I know this person ... this monster shot at you, too. I'm so glad you're okay."

Ann grimaced. The sound and even the taste of the air when the bullets zinged past her came to mind. She shivered at the memory and breathed slowly to calm her nerves. She had been scared to death. She and Logan were the lucky ones. Why did Webb have to get shot? She felt nauseous. *Survivor's guilt?*

"It's okay." Ann patted Tia's arms. She wished she could offer more now—an explanation, a reason for this horror, a solution to make everything better again. But she knew it would be futile. There were no answers. "I know what you mean, Tia. It's so unfair."

Tia nodded, her strawberry blond curls bouncing with the movements. She wiped her nose again.

"Ann," Logan said, urgency lacing his tone. He nodded with his chin toward the door. This was the third time he'd tried to hasten their departure. His voice and the intensity of his stare cut through her senses, and she swam from her fog to assess him.

Except for the telltale signs of concern, his expression was impossible to read. His face revealed nothing at all. It was blank. He didn't seem annoyed or angry with her, merely anxious, restless to get going, to return to an environment he could control.

She wanted to stay at the hospital until Webb could walk out on his own, but that was nonsensical. She'd spent a miserable night trying to sleep and worrying about her friend and partner. Before that, she had tried to convince Logan she needed to see Tia. To be there for her. Finally, after reaching Tia by phone and ascertaining Webb's status, she had agreed with Logan to wait until Webb was through surgery and somewhat stabilized.

Besides, Logan had convincingly argued, they shouldn't leave Ginny and Ann's mother with only Barrett at the house at night for protection. Not until they had a better idea of the threat. Hearing that logic, she had stopped arguing. The call that Webb was through surgery had come around 8:15 a.m. as they ate a silent breakfast of pancakes Delores McCarthy made.

By 10 a.m., Don had arrived, saying he wasn't on shift that day and would be there with Barrett as long as Logan needed him to stay.

Glancing at Logan now, Ann registered his patience was running short. He was determined to get out of there and return home.

He was right. They needed to leave. They had been there two hours comforting Tia and talking to the police assigned to guard Webb's room. At this point, there still were no suspects, and police were scrambling for leads.

"You're sure your parents will be here soon to keep you company?" Ann asked.

Tia nodded, and locks of her hair brushed onto her red, puffy face. Ann reached over and brushed them away as she stared at her friend. She leaned in to hug her again. "Remember, you have Logan's cell number. If you need anything, or there are any changes, call me."

She stood to go but turned back. "And Tia, if Sam ever shows up or calls, give him Logan's number. Tell him to call me immediately." Ann had tried unsuccessfully to reach Sam all morning. Calls to the CRS office had proven futile also, as Claire reported having no idea of Sam's whereabouts.

He'll have a hard time explaining this callousness.

Once outside the ICU waiting room, Ann sensed Logan tensing. A glance told her there was no imminent threat. It was just his anxiety to get out of there. To go home. They had taken a risk, one he hadn't agreed with. She owed it to him to cooperate as best she could. If someone was after them, a wounded Webb would be the perfect lure.

They turned a hallway corner. She looked up and down the corridor. They were only three doors away from the end of the long passage where a red exit sign indicated a door to the fire stairs. A man in sweat pants and a hospital gown moved toward them pushing an IV pole with one hand and holding his other hand at his side as though dealing with pain. His head was wrapped in white bandaging and his nose was black and blue. Otherwise, the corridor was empty in the direction they headed.

The nurses' station was about sixty feet behind them in the opposite direction, opening to the right of the hallway like a wide-open suite composed of only half walls and counters. Beside the station, a red-haired woman in a white lab coat talked with a gray-haired man in scrubs, both with their backs toward her and Logan.

"Relax," Ann said. "You'll be home with Ginny shortly." *We'll be safe.* But no closer to finding out who shot Webb or attacked her earlier.

"Can't come soon enough for my comfort," he said as he moved her along.

As they drew closer to the end of the corridor, Logan suddenly emitted a painful sound as though the air had been sucked out of him in one fell swoop. In her peripheral vision, she saw him falter, and a blur of movement beside him. In a panic, she turned to him and watched the man in the hospital gown pull a cop's metal baton away from Logan's gut to then smack it into his head.

The guy had been hiding it under the gown. That's why he looked like he was holding his side!

In the split second of shock before the creep was on her, she froze, watching Logan go down with a barely audible syllable of pain.

She tried to dodge the thug's grip, but it was too late.

Scrambling sideways, crashing into the wall in her haste to get away, she was seized by a thick arm viciously circling her neck and thrusting her back against a solid chest. Her air was cut off. With it went her ability to scream. She would have staggered, perhaps fallen, if it hadn't been for his hold on her.

"Gotcha." Satisfaction oozed from his voice as he wrenched open the fire exit door. "You won't get away this time."

Terror snaked through her core as he used a choke hold on her throat to haul her along. She tried again to scream, but nothing came out.

Even as panic gripped her, she registered that the whole attack in the hallway had taken a few heartbeats. That's all. Chances are, no one at the nurses' station saw or heard a thing. Given the whack the guy had given Logan on the side of the head, it seemed doubtful Logan would be able to get up for a while. *Please let him be okay.*

Her captor was strong and probably twice her weight, she realized with anguish as she guzzled in shallow bits of air, and her nails grabbed uselessly into the fabric of his shirt. Still, she tried to struggle, squirming her body and thrashing her hips about with as much force as her awkward position allowed.

He maneuvered her into a stairwell then grabbed her around the waist and forced her across the landing to descend the steps with him.

The stairwell was warmer, no doubt because the door blocked the air-conditioning. With a sickening feeling, she realized that same door would probably block all sound, too. The cinder-block walls and uncarpeted concrete further made it a place she doubted many people would tread today, if ever. *Please be with me. Save me!*

"Hold still or I'll finish you right here," he snarled as a waft of his body odor overwhelmed her senses. Tobacco and sweat. Just like the creep outside the convenience store!

She felt the terrifying cold of sharp metal press against the skin on her neck. *A knife!* She dropped her hands, afraid to move lest he mistake any movements as trying to fight him. She registered the thought that this guy also had the same height and build as the man who had attacked her outside the convenience store.

"Please ..." she rasped, but the word barely came. Her throat was too constricted. She tried again, forcing the words out. "Please, I won't fight. Don't hurt me." Her plea sounded pitiful.

"You've been a pain in my side, lady." He continued hauling her down the steps. "You broke my nose."

Panic twisted through her gut at the angry edge in his voice. She had no idea what she'd ever done to this man, but if she was a pain in the side to him, it would be a logical next step for a creep like this to end the pain. No matter how she cooperated, no matter what she promised or did, the end result looked like it would be the same.

"What do you want?" she rasped between ragged breaths. "I haven't done anything."

Terror prevented her from thinking clearly as he dragged her down the steps. Then a thought struck— *what you're doing isn't working. Do the opposite!*

So, she did. Rather than stiffen her spine and try to stay upright, she did the reverse. *What was there to lose?* If she fell and broke a bone or two, that would slow them down and give Logan time to find her, wouldn't it? At least it beat being hauled straight to her death without making an effort.

She went limp, deactivating every muscle holding her upright, sagging like gelatin on the spot. The man was thrown off balance from her deadweight. He gripped harder, wrenching her head and neck in an awkward—and painful—angle. The effort thrust them both forward, and they tumbled at least five steps.

In the fall, he cursed and lost his grip, crashing over her and coming to a stop on the landing, one step below where her feet sprawled. He bellowed something about his knee and promised she would pay gravely for this.

In the fall, she'd banged her right elbow and hip into the wall, landing on her bottom.

He'd fallen ahead of her on the stairwell, so she scrambled to go back up from where they had come. She felt his fingers grasping at her foot. She kicked at him, breaking free when his loose hospital gown got in his way.

Heart pounding, she yelled, "Help!" as she staggered backward hurriedly up the steps, too afraid to take her eyes off the hooligan. "I've been attacked! Help me!"

Behind her the door opened. "Ann!"

Logan!

At the sound of his voice, she threw a quick glance over her shoulder to see him bent over at the top of the steps, holding a hand to the side of his head. He wore a grimace like he was battling intense pain.

"Get the police!" she yelled. "The guy has a knife."

As she yelled, a sound came from behind her. She looked back to see the thug scramble down the stairs. From his stagger, it was clear his knee was damaged.

"He's getting away! Logan ..." She jerked her gaze back to see he had slumped to the floor at the stop of the steps, the pain making him curl like a shrimp.

LOGAN WATCHED Ann enter the examining room carrying two cups of coffee from the vending machine immediately outside the door. She wore a brace around her neck. He could see wisps of skin turning purple. The doctor had said she would be sore for a while, but she could discontinue the brace when it suited her. When Logan thought about how close they had come to that creep disappearing with her ...

He returned his attention to Michael Redding, the police detective that had spent the last twenty minutes questioning him. Prior to that, he'd been examined by a doctor while Redding revisited the scene with Ann.

He was tired of perching on the exam table and tired of the hospital. *We should have been on the road two hours ago.*

"Well, Mr. Kassell, those are all my questions for now. I'm afraid we don't have a lot to go on yet. As you know, we give special attention to objects, footprints, fingerprints, scuff marks, other traces that show activity or presence of persons at the scene. Unfortunately, we found only a few fingerprints, but I doubt they'll be helpful. More than likely they came from people that have used the stairwell for the past several months. Same with the IV he was pushing."

"I understand."

"And there just isn't enough evidence that the shots fired yesterday morning at you two and the attack at the convenience store and then here in the hospital are related."

Ann startled. "Not enough evidence? Surely you see how all this is tied together? The guy was the same height and build. He smelled the same! I can't be certain but his voice could have been the same, too."

The detective nodded. "I am keeping that in mind, for now. It's likely there is a tie. However, the incidents are circumstantial. Until we can pinpoint a target and a motive, I'm afraid we'll be guessing in the dark."

Ann's shoulders dropped, and she muttered an impatient sound under her breath.

Logan, however, wasn't ruffled by the detective's comments. Redding was right, there was no clear motive. Until they knew that, little headway would be made in this case. The motive would only reveal itself to Ann or him in time. In a flat voice, he repeated to the detective, "I understand."

Ann looked at him with incomprehension, but remained quiet.

"In the meantime," the detective added, "I'll be continuing the investigation beyond the preliminary stage. I'll make inquiries. Talk to the attendant at the convenience store that redirected you, but I'm guessing that guy is only guilty of being oblivious of what's going on around him. The attack on you, Ms. McCarthy, is considered aggravated assault. And, we certainly intend to investigate who shot your business partner, Mr. Hollis. My gut says when we identify the guy, we'll know who attacked you as well. Our Special Investigations Squad is composed of several highly educated and skilled detectives. We'll do our best."

Logan moved to drape his legs over the edge of the table. "Why is the Special Investigations Squad involved?" He had already explained to the detective that his understanding of the Baltimore police network came from his work as LubeRoyal's head of security. He had made it a point to get to know the police officers in whose purview LubeRoyal fell. He'd never met Detective Redding before but knew the squad was made up of dedicated individuals.

"Our unit is responsible for special or extraordinary investigations such as cases involving government officials or other officers or departments." He hesitated, and his jaw firmed as though he was about to add something he found distasteful. "Or as in this case, one with high media interest. These kinds of cases have the public rather concerned. Folks want to feel comfortable going to the hospital and with Lube-Royal in their midst."

High media interest. No wonder the detective had looked displeased. What's more, if high media interest described the situation surrounding LubeRoyal right now, then Tate must be furious.

"Keep your cell phone handy, Mr. Kassell," the detective said, rising from the lone chair in the room, "in case I have further questions. His gaze shifted to Ann. "I'll need to be able to reach you as well, Ms. McCarthy. "How long do you think you'll be at Mr. Kassell's side?"

Before she could respond, Logan cut in. "As long as it takes. You can reach her through me."

Ann flicked him another look. This one was definitely curious.

After the detective left, Ann handed Logan a cup of coffee and dropped into the vacated chair. "Mom and I can't stay with you indefinitely. You said yourself that it might disrupt Ginny."

Ginny. His innocent kid sister. He hated that the very job he had hoped would secure her future with him was putting her in possible jeopardy. He wanted to provide her with security, stability, routine. Instead, she was now a prisoner at the cabin, spending time with a woman she barely knew. What's more, her school life had been disrupted.

Ann looked at him expectantly, so he waved off her concern. "She'll have to adapt. You'll stay with us until this mess is resolved." He took a sip of the coffee and immediately spit it back into the cup. "Ugh, this is awful." He started to climb off the examining table but dropped back at the pain in his side. Ann stood and stepped closer, but he raised a stopping hand. He braced himself before trying again. This time, succeeding. "Come on, we're going home where we can have a decent cup of coffee."

"You can't leave! The doctors said you should stay overnight for observation."

He opened the door and gestured for her to proceed. "The optimum word being *should*. They've wrapped my ribs and given me pain meds. What I need now is a good night's rest. We both know I won't get it here. Besides, the guy who attacked you has not been found. He could still be in the hospital waiting to try again. They have security on Webb, but not you."

"I know, but—"

"I'm not letting you drive back to the cabin alone, and I doubt you want to spend the night in a chair like that." He pointed to where she'd been sitting.

She sighed. "Okay, but only if you promise we'll stop at the front desk and request—or bribe or whatever it takes—to get a guard to retrieve your car from the parking garage."

Now *that* was a good idea. They couldn't do enough contingency planning as far as he was concerned. He smiled. "It's a deal."

Twenty minutes later they were on Route 70, joining the stream of traffic heading west out of Baltimore. The sky was a beautiful pastel blue dotted with random smatterings of white clouds, and traffic was moving along well. Ann was driving, so Logan was free to think. But mostly what he thought about was how hard it was to concentrate, thanks to the pain killers they'd given him.

After a long silence, Ann said, "A penny for your thoughts."

Tate's possible involvement in all this had been on his mind. Instead, he asked, "You still determined to defend Sam? Or Aiden for that matter?"

From atop the brace, her head rolled in slow motion toward him and their eyes met for the briefest second before she returned her gaze to the road.

"I still don't see any motive for Aiden to be involved in something like this." She adjusted the rearview mirror. "But yes, I'm willing to entertain the highly unlikely possibility that he might be involved. Sam too, for that matter." She hesitated. "Somehow."

That, at least, is progress. He shot her a quick, searching look and was struck by how attractive her profile was, brace and all. *Had he noticed that before?* As for her comment, she didn't appear to be hiding anything. No flinching, no telltale signs of having said something merely to appease him. Still, it must have been hard for her to admit. The least he could do is lighten the moment. "You'll entertain the possibility? Not the probability?"

She frowned. "Don't push it."

"Fair enough. We'll talk in possibilities. So why do you now think it possible Sam could be involved?"

She made a quick sound of annoyance. "Highly, unlikely possibility, remember?"

Logan grinned at the clarifier.

"I don't know," Ann continued with a shrug, which, in turn, prompted her to grimace as though from pain. "I already told you about his situation with his wife and the women he's pursued before, during and after the break-ups."

"Other men cheat on their wives, but that doesn't make them criminals. Or for that matter, potential murderers. Cowards and quitters and cheaters, yes. People I don't want to associate with, yes. But not criminals and murderers."

"I know," Ann bit her lip as she set the cruise control, "but Webb and I have seen Sam pushing the edge when it comes to business ethics. Striking more and more deals without us, too."

Logan watched her brows scrunch together before she continued.

"Now that I think about it, the last few contracts were solidified without us because we always had something else scheduled. Sam could have asked our assistants about our schedules, but he didn't. I hadn't thought about that before."

Interesting. Her comment prompted him to think about his own situation. He wished these pain meds weren't in him so he could think better. But he was certain LubeRoyal's contract with CRS was the only one involving security Tate had ever signed without his involvement.

"Please understand ..." Ann began. In Logan's peripheral vision, he caught her turning her head as much as the brace would allow to look at him. He caught her gaze before she returned hers to the road. But it was long enough to see splotches of pink bloom on her face. "... I would have agreed to work with your company anyway. I would have signed the contract. In fact, I'm very impressed with you—" She broke off and scrunched her face. "I mean with LubeRoyal of course."

He stifled a grin. "Of course." Too bad she hadn't stopped after the 'impressed with you' comment. He would have liked that better because he sure was getting more impressed with her as he spent time with her. Family and friends were clearly more important to her than what he'd thought at first. The way she had fretted over her mother and now consoled her friend, Tia. He liked that. What's more, she was rocking the jeans her mother had brought with her. Much better than that power suit. She looked more like an Anna Grace all the time. He wondered how she'd look in a pair of wellies as she hiked the fields around his house. Logan shook his head. Where had that thought come from? And when? How had the switch flipped such that he now saw this woman not only as very astute and strong, but tender-hearted and compassionate as well? *Must be the meds.* Then again ...

"Tell you what," Logan groaned. "My head is not functioning at full capacity. We'll have to table this conversation until later. Right now, I want to get home and crash. There's a couch there calling for me."

Ann nodded. "No worries. Feel free to lie down as soon as we get home. I imagine Ginny and Mom will want someone new to talk to, so I'll handle that. I'll update Barrett and Don, too."

"You're probably right. I told Ginny to stay off the Internet. And the TV. I didn't want them getting upset with what the news media reports."

"Oh dear." Ann inched her gaze to him and rolled her eyes. "I wonder what in the world they're doing for entertainment."

"Maybe I was a little too strict, but I didn't want your mother getting upset either. I assumed you didn't want her to realize how close those bullets were to hitting you."

"Good assumption."

Logan looked at the mountains in the distance—their destination. He closed his eyes, wondering what would come next. He felt dopey and tired. Too tired. And listless.

The rest of the drive home went by in a blur.

CHAPTER SEVEN

Ann opened her eyes to darkness. Her second night in Logan's bedroom. Inching to a sitting position so as not to irritate her neck, she let her vision acclimate to the shadows and varied shapes in the room. She knew its layout and its appearance by heart. It had the stamp of him from wall to wall. Not perfect or designed to impress but pleasingly practical with a comfortable masculinity that both men and women would find welcoming. Here, the furniture and décor were quality and presented a works-together vibe, but one could play a board game on its bedspread and brush crumbs onto the floor without reproach.

Beside her, Delores McCarthy rasped the breathing of someone in a deep sleep. Her mother had to be tired. When Ann and Logan arrived home the night before, they had expected to be greeted at the door by two very concerned and annoyed family members. Instead, Ginny and Delores had tossed them a "Hi" and "Hey there," from opposite sides of the couch where they sat facing one another, playing an intense game of Rummy.

According to Barrett, they had been playing for hours. Before that, Delores had taught Ginny how to knit. Earlier in the day, the two made a delicious pot roast and apple dumplings.

Fortunately, the lights had been turned low throughout the house, allowing she and Logan to move through the shadows on the edges of the rooms, attracting no concerning attention. Rather than interrupt their fun, Logan and Ann had briefed Barrett about the incident at the hospital then ate leftovers. Within the hour, Logan crashed on the couch and Ann headed off to bed.

Later, she had woken at midnight, discovering herself alone in the bed. When she went searching for her mother, she found the exterior door leading from the living room to the front veranda cracked open. She inched through, careful not to wake Logan on the fold-out couch a mere eight feet away. Her mother was sitting in the dark, staring at the sky. Ann had tracked her gaze to see a wide panorama of stars. She felt like she was in a planetarium. Rather than pull her mother from the spectacular view, she folded into a chair beside her, soaked in the beauty, and exchanged a few poignant moments of conversation about normal things. Things that had nothing to do with explosions and threats and fears.

Now, in the dim light, she studied her mother. Yes, she would probably sleep for several hours yet.

She probably should sleep longer, too. She read the digital clock. 4:20 a.m. Too early to rise. But what did that matter when she was wide awake? It was the anxiety. In the span of an instant her mind sifted through the events of the past couple days. Memories of that thug hauling her into the hospital stairwell swished through her mind, and she swallowed a lump against crying, managing to keep the tears at bay. She refused to feel weak. Like a victim. There were others to think about. Webb. Her mother. Ginny.

And Logan. When she had watched him falter on the stairwell landing, her heart lurched. She shook her head thinking about it now. Must have been the fervor of the moment or the fact he had been her protector for the past two days. It couldn't be more than that. She barely knew him.

She moved her head right. Left. A little stiffness but not pain. She ignored the brace, let it remain on the nightstand. No need to raise unnecessary concern.

Gingerly, she climbed out of bed and padded quietly toward the kitchen. The house was still. A medieval, pre-technology, pre-moving-vehicle quiet. Don had gone home, but Barrett was still there, sleeping upstairs. Ginny was in her room. Everyone was safe in bed. It brought her comfort. *How long will it last?*

With the aid of the dull illumination spilling from the light over the stove in the kitchen, she tiptoed past Logan sleeping in the living room. Stubborn man. He had insisted on sleeping on the couch again, leaving his bed for her and her mother. If anyone should have spent a night in a comfortable bed, it was him.

Once in the kitchen, she debated: herbal tea or coffee? She'd seen both in the cupboard yesterday. Did she want to attempt more rest? Or was it a doomed undertaking, and she may as well pump herself with caffeine to face the day?

She opted for coffee.

While it brewed, she assessed the expansive kitchen and eating area. Beautiful. Tasteful. Logan's skills as a carpenter were evident. The cabinets were done in a soft gray, and the shiplapped walls an off-white. It had a country kitchen vibe to it with rugs and other décor accents in black, indigo, white, gold, and wood tone.

It was perfect. She couldn't imagine changing a single thing.

Get a grip on yourself, Ann. Why wonder if the place suits you? She groaned. Because it had begun to feel like safety, that's why. Because, oddly enough, she had already started getting used to driving beside its owner. Eating with him. Caring what happened to him. "Don't go there," she mumbled sternly. She couldn't let involvement with a man distract her from her plans. Her mother needed her.

She startled when Logan's voice sounded out, his voice pitched low as if from grogginess. "Ummm, that coffee smells good. Mind if I join you?"

Ann turned to watch a drowsy, barefooted Logan enter the room, wearing gym trunks and an untucked T-shirt.

"Of course. It's your coffee. I hope I didn't wake you."

"I've been awake for a while," he said, but his droopy eyes suggested otherwise.

"How are you feeling?" she asked, with forced brightness, trying to push her earlier thoughts from her mind.

"Head is better. Side still hurts a little." He moved to the table and held his hand over his abs as he folded slowly into a chair, a grimace of discomfort crossing his face. "And you're welcome to anything in the kitchen you need. The whole house, for that matter."

She moved to the cupboard where she had found her cup, retrieved a second one, and poured his coffee. "You've been so generous. Your coffee, your food, your home." She hesitated. "Your protection. I'll never be able to repay you." She carried the cups to the table.

"I think you already have. Looks to me like my sister has found a true friend in your mother. I heard Ginny call her Nana Delores last night." He twisted his lips. "I never saw that one coming."

"Me either."

He rolled his head as though stretching out the night's stiffness. "I guess Ginny's desirous of more family. More people to love and to love her in return."

"I don't think I've seen my mother this happy for quite a while. After she and dad returned from Zimbabwe, she seemed content. Fine with not teaching anymore. Or doing missions. No pressure. No schedules. It never occurred to me she might miss mothering a young person. That always was her favorite role."

The edges of Logan's lips curled up. "You're lucky."

A pang of remorse shot through Ann's gut. She instinctively reached out to him. They were sitting close enough at the table that it took little effort to place her hand on his forearm. "I'm sorry. I didn't mean anything by that. I forgot—"

The moment she touched him, his eyes widened in surprise and his gaze slid down to where her fingers met his skin. After a moment, he lifted his gaze to meet hers again. His reaction to her touch was impossible to read, but clearly, he hadn't expected her to do it.

"It's okay," he said, his tone offering reassurance. "I know what you meant. I like to think that were it not for the drugs, mothering would have been my mom's primary focus, too."

They lapsed into silence, the only sound the hum of the refrigerator and an ember popping in what remained of last night's blaze in the fireplace.

Ann circled the top of her cup with her index finger. "So, what's next?

"What do you mean?"

She splayed her hands to include them, the kitchen, the house, everything. "What are we going to do next? I can't stay here forever. We have to figure out how to remove this threat." She tried to remain calm, to keep her voice from sounding panicky.

Logan scratched his head. "I've been racking my brain trying to pinpoint a motive. But we know so little. Problem is, I can't ask Don to be here all the time. Barrett either."

"I've wondered about that. If, Don is an EMT, how does he get so much free time? And what about Barrett's work?"

"Don works long hours when he's on shift. He gets several days off in a row. Barrett is between jobs right now. He's back in school to get his electrician's license. Both Don and Barrett also devote time to our consulting work."

"Consulting work?"

Logan nodded. "SEALS. We tend to stick together even after serving. We're hired to provide organizational support from time to time. Don is here a lot while I'm at LubeRoyal. He's much more involved than I am at this point."

Ann thought about that. "And you trust all the guys you work with?"

"With my life. And my confidences. These guys are used to learning and forgetting the more personal aspects of their brothers." He leaned back slowly, wincing once, and stretched his legs out under the table. "But to be honest, I think I'm about as involved as I want to get. I'll always provide an organizing center for them, here. It's the best place. Most equipped. But once my time with LubeRoyal is over, I want to get back into carpentry. That's my calling. What I'm supposed to do."

Ann blinked, not tracking his thought process. "Supposed to do? You make it sound like it's someone else's decision. Not your own."

He shrugged. "It's both actually. What has been placed on my heart is mine to choose or ignore. It's what I have an interest in. You voiced an interest in research journalism. That's what has been placed in you. Somehow, someway, you can serve people through doing that."

Ann swallowed. If that's true, then what she has been doing at CRS to secure money seemed very greedy. Self-serving. But she was doing it to save the farm to make her mother happy. *Did that make it wrong?* Was she assigning desire for a certain outcome and more money as higher importance than doing what her heart told her she should be doing? No, that couldn't be ... she had expectations placed on her. Demands. Responsibilities. *Didn't she?* Logan's voice cut into her thoughts.

"Look, I can't explain the explosion at LubeRoyal and how all this is linked together, but it's clear you and Webb are targets. We need to get in touch with Sam. Feel him out. Figure out if he's involved in this or if he might be a target as well. We know you got that warning outside your office building while Sam was inside. Then, the guy grabbed you at the convenience store and the hospital and referred to the earlier incidents. I, for one, want to know if Sam is the one who hired this creep."

Ann studied him while he talked. He seemed to be thinking, planning out loud as much as he was talking to her.

He must have felt the weight of her gaze, because he looked up from his coffee. "You think it was the same guy, but you were on the ground the first time. The guy at the convenience store and the one at the hospital had a similar smell. Could be the same man. You said he was about the same size. As for those bullets, they seemed random. They didn't care if they hit me, too. Then Webb got shot. So, the main target seems to be you or your company but as associated with my company."

Ann remained quiet.

"As for LubeRoyal, I feel I'm doing it as much of a service by removing the targets and keeping the perpetrator away from the facility." He took another sip. "At least, that's what I'll argue with Tate in the end."

Ann gasped. *Moving them away* "Does that mean you're hoping to lure the creep here?"

"No," he leaned forward, winced again, and held his palm to her. "I'm not knowingly putting you in jeopardy. I wouldn't do that to you. To anyone. Especially your mom or Ginny. It's just that you seem to be a target. If they—he, they, whomever—are determined to find you, I would much rather it be here where I can help. Where I'm fully equipped and can control the environment rather than on the streets in Baltimore or D.C."

"How do you know the target isn't LubeRoyal? The events started there. It can't be ruled out."

"True. I've not closed any doors. But as I said, I've brainstormed this until my head feels like it might explode. I can't see how damaging LubeRoyal would personally hurt me so badly that it would benefit anyone who might have a vendetta against me or my work with the SEALs. No, I think the company is a secondary concern in all this."

Ann sighed. "I still feel bad I had to abandon LubeRoyal after the first briefing. Helping them is my job at times like this."

"You can't help them if you get hurt," Logan said. "Besides, you set the stage for a steady flow of truthful, forthcoming information. If Tesslar ruins it now, it's not your fault." He paused. "Are you saying you'd rather go back to Baltimore? Do you not feel safe here? Surely you saw yesterday how we can't rely on the police? They're good, but their resources are stretched thin, and it's going to take them a while to investigate."

"Of course, I feel safe here. It ... well," she looked around, "... it seems to be very highly fortified."

He grinned and his blue eyes sparkled. "What do you mean?"

"The walls are extremely thick and the windows particularly thick, like they're some sort of specialized safety glass. You have a monitor hidden inside a cupboard, cameras around the property, and a rather sophisticated computer system in your office. Plus, there are a lot of interior doors. Behind which, I'm guessing, are weapons for fortification, and supplies for long-term stay."

He wiped a hand down the morning stubble on his chin. "Is it that obvious?"

"Not really. Just basing it on some things you said about your consulting work. Are you preparing for the worst? You know, like one of those dooms-day preppers?"

"I've fortified my cabin with a lot of safety features other people don't have. And yes, I have in my possession a significant amount of long-term food stored away. But am I worried about it? No. Is it for doomsday? No. I'm relying on my wits and my training to protect Ginny and me. But likewise, I don't start out on a long trip with an empty tank. Some strategic planning is always a good idea. I'm sure you know that from the line of work you're in currently."

She liked that he said 'currently.' A nod to his understanding—perhaps even agreement?—with the change in career she planned one day. "Why all the special fortifications?"

He huffed a short syllable of dismay. "You can't do the work we're doing here without ruffling some feathers along the way. Although it's extremely rare."

"Yet you're certain no one out there has a vendetta against you?"

"None I can think of. Don couldn't pinpoint anyone either. But am I certain? No. We can never be certain. Things are always changing."

Ann smiled. "One of my roommates likes to say 'change is the only constant.' Speaking of which, I really ought to call one of them today. Let them know I'm fine and that mom is with me."

"Sure. Call them later. Just keep it vague. What time do they get up?"

"Rhea would be up now. She does an early shift at the paper on Wednesdays."

Maneuvering his legs from beneath the table, Logan placed his hand on his side and stood. He disappeared into the living room for a moment, returning with his cell phone in his hand. He handed it to her then picked up their cups. "Call her while I refresh these."

Less than five minutes later, Ann clicked off the call and stood, closing her fingers around the phone. "Rhea said Sam hasn't called. But Aiden has. Several times. She said he sounds unhinged. He called Miranda, too. He's desperate to talk to me as soon as possible. She's going to text you the number he gave her."

As she handed back the phone, it pinged announcing a text had come in.

A FARAWAY LOOK had descended in her eyes when she mentioned Aiden, and Logan didn't like it. This was someone from her past. Her *past*.

Why should that concern him? No, he only felt unease about this Aiden chump because the guy hit her once. He despised that behavior in men. She deserved better. *Much better*.

Logan looked at the phone then back at her without accepting the device. "Then we'll grant his wish. We'll go into the mudroom and call him on speaker phone. The acoustics are good. He'll never know he's on speaker. With the door shut, it won't wake anyone still sleeping." He moved his hand in a beckoning motion and headed toward the mudroom off the side of the kitchen.

She followed. "What? You mean now?"

He turned to stare at her. She sounded hesitant. A multitude of emotions flickered in her eyes but none he could isolate. She remained unreadable.

He shrugged. "It's as good a time as any, isn't it? Besides, what do you care if you wake him?

Ann shook her head, stray wisps of hair falling onto one side of her face. She brushed them back carelessly. "I ... I don't care. I just don't know if I'm prepared to ... if I want to talk to him."

She was talking faster, and her breathing had quickened. Was she hiding something? Something she didn't want him to hear?

Or was he being callous about how she might feel right now? After all, the guy had slugged her once. She bore no physical scars that he could see, but that slug probably caused an emotional scar that might never go away.

His gut told him to trust her. He *wanted* to trust her. Without thinking it through, he reached out and gently cupped the side of her cheek. "It will be fine. He's only on the phone. He doesn't know where you are. I'll be right here beside you."

The moment elongated as she tilted her head and leaned her cheek into his hand.

His heart rate accelerated. *Stop*, his mind counseled. She's seeking comfort, assurance. That's all. Right now, she would have leaned into anyone who could provide it. He was about to remove his hand when she shifted. She looked unfazed by the moment. Like her mind was focused solely on the task ahead.

With brisk, firm nods, she said, "You're right. Let's do this. At least we might figure out if he's involved or not."

They proceeded to the mudroom, a small room filled with an unorganized jumble of wellies and scattered shoes that looked to be walking over themselves. Coats and umbrellas hung from racks, a counter held a pink school bag and several flashlights, and a white board announced two activities that were already out of date. Logan eased the door shut.

The phone rang four times before a groggy male voice said a wary, "Hello," as if it were as much a question as a greeting.

"Aiden. It's Ann. You wanted to talk to me?" She sounded like she was speaking with all the firmness she could muster.

"Ann! Where the blazes have you been? Why didn't you call me sooner? I'm sure Rhea and Miranda told you I've been trying to reach you."

Her shoulders stiffened at his words but her gaze lingered on Logan. "It's a long story. How long have you been out, and what do you want?" Her voice took on a brusqueness.

"Ahh. Ann, I can hear your annoyance. You're still mad. I guess I don't blame you. But I've changed. You'll see. A little time together and you'll get to know the new me. A newer, better me. I've been out for three weeks—"

"Aiden, I'm not mad." Her gaze shifted to the floor. "I'm not upset about how long you've been out. I was only curious."

"I wanted to call you right away, but I wanted to get my act together before we talked."

"And you think you've got it together now?" Her question came out in a tone that suggested skepticism, and she flinched at her own words.

"I'm working on it, but things have changed. I wasn't even out of the correctional facility twenty-four hours before some guy—some stranger—called me. His number was blocked. Said he knew about you and your work. Wanted to know if I'd like to make some quick money. I guess ex-cons have a reputation for needing funds as soon as they're back in society." A syllable of exasperation came over the line. "Which isn't all that wrong, I suppose."

Logan watched Ann's face pale as she lifted her free hand to her chest. He moved closer and gestured a circling motion to say 'get more information.'

"Who was he? What did he want you to do?"

"If I knew who he was, don't you think I would have told you? I have no idea. He said he knows a way we could use you to get rich."

"Use me? In what manner?" Her voice was still steady, but Logan noticed her hand beginning to shake.

"I don't know. I was so startled, I cut him off. Said I wasn't interested. I told you, I've changed, Ann. You'll see."

As Aiden said this last bit, Logan hurriedly swiped clean the white board.

Ann read the words he wrote and repeated them. "When did he call?"

"I don't know. Early last week, I guess."

"Last week and you're just now telling me?"

"But that's just it. Sunday night some guy showed up at my room ... I, ah, well, I'm renting a room in a small boarding house. For now. It's only temporary. It'll take me a while to get my investments together ..." He paused as though waiting for Ann to comment. When she didn't he continued, "Anyway, that's why I started calling you. I mean, how did this jerk know where I lived? I haven't been out that long. I can't be sure, but I think it was the same guy who called last week. When I asked him about it, he acted like he didn't know what I was talking about. But I think it was an act."

Ann watched Logan change the white board again. She read, "What did he look like?"

"Tall. Pale skin. I think he was blond. The rest of him was all cloak and dagger stuff. Dark sunglasses, a hat, and trench coat."

Logan wrote, "Tattoos? Piercings?"

Ann said, "Did he have any distinguishing marks, like tattoos? A mustache or beard? Piercings? Anything?"

"Not that I recall. Like I said, most of him was covered. I watched him climb into a van when he left. No markings on the side."

"What did he want?" Ann asked.

"He wanted to know how he could find you. He acted casual. You know, less threatening. Almost professional. He claimed to be an old friend. Wanted to know where you might hang out if not at your apartment or your mom's in West Virginia."

Logan watched Ann rub her forehead. His heart twisted for her. He could practically taste his anger at this assailant.

She licked her lower lip. "He said that?" Her free hand dropped from her chest to her front. She wrapped it around her middle as if to hug herself. "He knows I have an apartment and where I go to see my mother?"

"I told him I didn't know and wouldn't share contact information with him anyway. Not without talking to you."

Ann shifted to lean her body against the wall. Logan grabbed the coats off a straight-back chair and pushed it to her. She dropped onto it.

"Ann?" Aiden's anxious voice rose higher. "You still there?"

She blinked. "I'm here. Anything else?"

"Just that I miss you."

Her gaze lifted to meet Logan's. "Aiden don't."

"I'd like to see you. Show you how I've changed. We could even get together with your co-workers, if you like. I never understood Webb all that well, but I always liked Sam a lot. I've been thinking about calling him."

"Aiden, call whomever you want, but I'm not—"

"Ann," he rushed on, "I've been going to church. I knew you'd like that."

Ann closed her eyes. "You have to do that for yourself, not for me. Besides, sitting in a church doesn't make anyone a better person. It's what's inside that ... never mind." She paused as though she were collecting her thoughts. "Aiden, I'm happy for you. Happy you're out. Happy you've changed. Happy you feel good about your future. But I've already told you it's a future that no longer includes me. I've moved on. If there's nothing else, I'm going to hang up."

"What?" He sounded deflated. "Oh, sure. For now. We'll talk again some other time. I won't give up until you see how I've changed. How can I reach you? There wasn't any number displayed with this call."

Logan had already erased the board and now scribbled a large, 'no!'

She tilted her head in acknowledgement. "You can't, Aiden. Look I've gotta go."

"Ann, be careful. If this was the same guy both times, then maybe you should talk to the police. And call me—"

"Goodbye, Aiden." She clicked off the call.

For a moment, they stared at each other. If Logan were to guess, he'd say it was turmoil he read on her face. A man she had once loved and trusted, one who then hit her, was telling her about another man who seemed to have intentions to hurt her in some way.

"Come on," he offered her a hand to help her stand. "Let's go to the kitchen and talk about this. I think I'm going to make you a cup of decaf."

The kitchen remained dimly lit. Sunrise in Maryland, even on top of a mountain, generally didn't arrive until about 6 a.m.

Logan filled the tea kettle with water and put it on the stove then loaded a French press with loose, decaffeinated coffee.

Ann dropped onto a stool at the counter facing him.

He studied her. Clearly, she was shaken, but was it because of Aiden or what she'd learned from him? "You okay?"

"About what Aiden said? No, and I'm sure glad you brought Mom here. About Aiden himself?" She waved a hand as though swiping away everything about him. "He belongs in my past and that's it." She paused. "Isn't he unbelievable? After what he did … Hitting me. Emotionally manipulating me. Destroying my trust. Then, breaking the law and spending time in prison. He knows I no longer have feelings for him and even less respect." Her voice was calm, convincing. "I don't understand why he would still want me in his life anyway."

I do, Logan thought. *You're intelligent, beautiful, witty, and interesting to be around. He was a fool to let you go. He already had a fortune at his side and didn't even see or respect it.*

"You heard him talk," Ann continued. "He's so sure of himself and his ability to get what he wants. It's not confidence, it's brashness, almost obnoxiousness. Makes it easy to see why he thought he could manipulate the law and get away with it."

As Logan poured boiling water into the French press, he chuckled under his breath. "Yeah, the guy does sound like he could talk the hind leg off a donkey. Must have surprised him when both a she-donkey and a legal-donkey kicked back."

Ann looked up startled. Her lips curled and her face lit up. As though a dam had been opened, she pulled back her head and after the briefest glimmer of pain, laughed. Long gales of glee, one after the other. In seconds, she was wiping tears from her face even as she continued to shake with laughter. Logan could hear the tension pouring from her, released by this moment of bland mirth.

As she laughed, he finished pressing her decaf. He poured a cup and placed it in front of her. She reached out and touched his hand. He froze on the spot, waiting to hear her through.

"Thank you," she said, her voice almost a whisper. "For so many things. For helping and sheltering Mom and me. For listening. For considering my point of view in this whole confusing mess. Most of all for lightening the moment just now when I needed it most."

For some reason, her words stirred something in him. To Logan, it looked like her eyes sparkled, and he lost himself in it. He bent his head slowly, giving her time to back away. *Please,* he thought, *she needs to turn away.* Because I can't stop myself from kissing her. Because she is fragile right now, and I don't want to take advantage of her vulnerability. Because relationships born in crises are a cliché, and they rarely last. Because her eyes are focused on me with forensic interest as though she trusts me implicitly. *For all these reasons, she needs to turn away.*

But she didn't. If anything, she leaned in to meet him midway. Her eyes closed and her lips parted, inviting him to follow through. Their lips met for a second. Then two. A sweet, gentle, oh-so-perfect elongated instant. The stillness of the morning wrapped around them, adding a touching poignancy to the moment.

When he pulled back, he noted daybreak poking through the gray pallor a sun-ray at a time and the familiar sounds of Ginny's fuzzy pink slippers padding quickly toward the kitchen.

CHAPTER EIGHT

"Please, Logan. Pah-lease."

Ann tried to keep from grinning as Ginny elongated the second entreaty, turning it into one of those pitiful, drawn-out requests for permission. If the pleas didn't work, surely the sad puppy dog eyes would.

Barrett had entered the kitchen seconds behind Ginny, so he'd heard the whole exchange, too. Ann shifted her gaze to look at him and noted that he openly wore the grin she fought to keep at bay.

Ginny moved as close into Logan as her little five-foot height would allow. "The other kids bring their parents and grandparents to school. I never have anyone to show off. You're always working. I want to take Nana Delores today. She's the closest thing to a grandmother I'll ever have. She promised to do a tribal dance she learned in Zimbabwe. Nobody's grandparents have ever done that before!"

To his credit, Logan did not interrupt. Did not say no. Instead, he sat there, a stoic expression on his face, hearing her out. Still, Ann saw concern in his eyes. No doubt his desire to keep Ginny safe warred with his desire to give her as normal a life as possible. Not for the first time, Ann admired his devotion to his sister. To family.

When Ginny finally paused, Logan rubbed his mouth and chin a few times as though contemplating.

Ginny must have thought he was about to respond in the negative because she ramped up her plea. "I've already missed two days of school. You can't keep me out forever. What if we just go for the afternoon? This way I can get the homework I've missed, and I'll still be there for history class. That way, Nana Delores can demonstrate her dance."

"Ginny, enough," Logan said. He softened both his face and his voice when he continued. "If I can figure out a way to make this happen, we'll do it. But you and Mrs. McCarthy are not going to school without protection. Problem is, I can't go today. I've got to check with my staff at LubeRoyal to make sure things are under control. We have a good system and good people, but I'm still responsible. Ginny, there also have been other things this week that happened that I can't get into. Matters that need my attention."

"I can take them," Barrett offered.

When all eyes turned to him, he shrugged. "I haven't been in a kids' school for years. It'll be fun."

Logan studied him. "Don't you have to get back?"

"Nah, not really. I'm between jobs since I'm studying electrical work now. Besides, I'm a bachelor, remember? That means I have to eat my own cooking. Trust me, what I cook can't hold a candle to what's come out of this kitchen in the past few days. I believe I heard beef stroganoff was on the menu tonight." He grinned sheepishly.

Ginny bounced with excitement. "Please say yes, Logan. Let Barrett take us."

Logan chuckled. "I'll call the school so they're not startled when two strangers arrive with you. But you stay in Barrett's site the whole time, you hear? First, you better make sure Mrs. McCarthy wants to accompany you. Her health is compromised, so let her set the pace without pushing her."

"Deal!" Ginny beamed. She threw her arms around her brother in a monstrous bear hug. "Thank you, Logan." When she let go, she immediately turned and hugged Barrett then Ann with equal force. "Thank you, Anna Grace."

Ann startled. "What did I do?"

Ginny shrugged. "You've made the place better. And Logan's more easy-going with you here. Besides, you're still going to help me with my research project, aren't you?"

"Of course, I am."

"Do you think Nana Delores will be awake soon? I can't wait to tell her!"

Ann tilted her head, pretending to think. "I don't think she'll mind you waking her for exciting news like this."

Ginny giggled and ran from the room.

Silence descended after her departure. Finally, Barrett broke it. "So, what's for breakfast?" he said as he rubbed his stomach.

THE EARLY AFTERNOON sun warmed the sky before Ann finally let herself ponder the kiss she shared with Logan. *The* kiss. The incredible, unexpected, electricity-magnetizing-the-air kiss. It had been wonderful. But what it meant and what seemed to be happening between them were outside her comfort zone. How could she think logically when she was surrounded with him? His house. His work. This whole situation—him and that fill-the-whole-room-with-his-presence way of his. Was she ready for a relationship again? And particularly, with Logan?

Then again, the familiarity and snugness that permeated the very walls of his home with them all tucked in it *was* very much in her comfort zone. She wanted that in her life. She'd just never thought it might come along now. In this place. In this way. She had a feeling she had plunged into a situation that was more than she had bargained for at the outset. But was that so bad?

And what had Logan been thinking when he kissed her? Had he put more than a moment of thought into it beforehand, or was it just a knee-jerk reaction brought on by the gratitude she expressed at that moment?

You're being ridiculous, she scolded herself. The only way to know the answer is to ask him. Yet people rarely could analyze their own feelings adequately. Besides, did she really want to ponder this to where it destroyed her memory of it?

She needed to get out of that house. To think more clearly.

Truth was, however, she was in no hurry. Sure, earlier in the week she had wanted to hurry back to her work and apartment. She had felt like an imposition here. A burden. She had wanted to seize control of her life and her own safety.

But that was before the creep grabbed her. The threat had been too real and too frightening. And the worst part was, she believed he wasn't done trying. They still had no ID on him. No motive. No rationale as to what spurred him to do what he had done.

No, if it meant keeping herself and her mother safer by staying put, then she would do that. Her mother seemed fine with the notion, too, judging by the comfort and peace she had voiced the night before when Ann found her sitting on the veranda.

She sighed and turned her attention back to the list of calls she needed to make that day. Using Logan's cell, she called her brother to let him know their mother was fine and how he could reach the two of them. Then she phoned Tia, learning Webb was holding his own. If he made it through the next few days without problems, doctors didn't think there would be any permanent damage. Next, she called both Rhea and Miranda, extending apologies for the clandestine nature of their interactions in the past few days. All the calls were brief, delivering need-to-know information only.

Next on her list were work contacts. First on that priority was Claire. The two talked about Webb for about twenty minutes. Like her, Claire liked and admired him. Ann could tell talking about Webb eased Claire's stress a bit. Claire assured her that building security had been tightened, but that at least two clients had expressed concern about CRS's work with them. Thereafter, Ann followed up by calling both clients to ease their worry.

The last name on her list was Sam. Claire had said Sam called in twice yesterday looking for her but hadn't called or come into the office yet today.

She exhaled slowly and punched in his number on Logan's cell phone. Earlier, Logan had handed her a small recording device, requesting she capture the conversation so he could listen to it later, too. She plugged it into the cell phone and turned it on. Ethically, she ought to inform Sam he was being recorded, but she reasoned, desperate times call for desperate measures. And at this point, she certainly owed more to Logan than she did to Sam. Besides, once Logan heard it, she planned to erase it.

He answered on the fourth ring. "Bromberg here."

"Sam, it's Ann."

"It's about time! Where are you? Are you all right?" He sounded both anxious and annoyed.

"I've been better. Given that someone has tried to shoot and kidnap me, I could be worse." She knew her tone was dry, sarcastic, but she didn't care.

"Kidnap! What are you talking about?"

Ann gripped the phone tighter. "First outside a convenience store a few hours after the initial shooting at LubeRoyal. Then again yesterday in the hospital when I went to see Webb."

He cursed. Then mumbled, "Yeah, I heard about Webb."

Ann flinched at the cavalier tone in his voice regarding Webb. It was a gun shot, not a stubbed toe. "Heard about him? You haven't gone to see him yet?"

"What? No, I ... ah ... had to be at LubeRoyal. Then here. Someone has to hold this place together, keep business on track ... and I had some personal matters to take care of."

"Personal matters?" She was quickly growing impatient with him. "Sam, people at our company are being attacked—" She stopped as a thought dawned on her. Her heart rate accelerated. "You're not worried about your own safety, are you? That's because you know something—"

"Where are you? We need to talk in person." His voice had changed to a gruff whisper.

"That's impossible. I'm at a location which I choose not to disclose over the phone. If you know anything—"

"You're still with that Kassell guy from LubeRoyal, aren't you?" A pause. Then, as though to himself, "That's good, I suppose. That'll be safer."

Ann gripped the phone tighter. "How did you know I ... Wait, safer than what?"

"Come on, Ann. Both companies know you left LubeRoyal together." His voice, so frenzied, almost hissing an instant before, was suddenly filled with a biting sarcasm. "Tate said Kassell has a place in central Maryland. In the mountains. I assume you're there."

Ann rubbed her forehead. That wasn't good. Had she and Logan been that transparent in their disappearance? If she ever made it out of this, she would have to set up a rumor control system for LubeRoyal. Then too, what was with Sam's behavior? He sounded mild and concerned one second then volatile and defensive the next. "Sam, what else do you know?"

He huffed. "What do you mean what do I know?"

Ann shook her head. In her time with Sam, she had learned the man repeated questions when cornered, and when he didn't want to provide an honest answer. "Someone has tried to kill Webb and me. Do you get the seriousness of this? I want to know who and why before they try again. I suspect it has something to do with our contract with LubeRoyal. I was going to tell you to be careful, too, but now it makes me wonder why you're not worried about your own—"

He mumbled something she couldn't catch. He continued louder, as though he had moved his mouth closer to the phone. "Look, I only wanted to know where you are to make sure you're safe. Things have gotten out of control here. I'm still trying to figure out what to do about it. How I can stop it." The latter sentence was softer again as though he were speaking to himself.

"Stop what? Sam, talk to me. Who or what are you talking about?"

"Look, Ann, I didn't do anything. You gotta believe me on this."

His words were rushed together as if he couldn't get them out fast enough. "Someone may have inadvertently—"

"Someone?"

He hesitated. "Yes, okay, Tracy. Are you satisfied? She seems to think she and I have a future. Apparently, she's told her brother this, too."

"What has that got to do with me? With Webb?" Silence again.

Ann pushed the phone to her ear. "Sam?"

"Look, I've got to go. Just keep a low profile for a while."

The phone disconnected.

SITTING IN HIS OFFICE, Logan clicked off his home line from talking with Detective Redding. He stretched and rolled his head in a circle. Redding had reported little. The casings found at the site of the shooting at LubeRoyal came from a 5.56 rifle; the attendant at the convenience store was clean and remembered little about the man who told him to redirect Ann when she left the restroom; and no one in the hospital had seen or heard anything unusual before, during, or after he and Ann were attacked.

Before that, Logan had spent most of the morning talking with Collier, various supervisors under his purview, and a couple department heads. The explosion was fully contained, damage repairs were underway, and the batch involved in the explosion was being replicated, although LubeRoyal would take a huge financial hit on it. The dead employee's funeral was Friday, and LubeRoyal was giving employees time-off with pay to attend. Rumors had enhanced the story to the point where public sentiment decided the whole incident was due to an environmentalist that had gone berserk, sabotaging LubeRoyal to make a statement. That was subject to change at any time, and supposition remained about what caused the explosion in the first place.

As far as his company's processes were concerned, the whole incident seemed to be a thing of the past. The problem was, there was still a killer on the loose. A relentless killer who, for whatever reason, kept bringing his vendetta to them.

Who was it? And, why would someone want to hurt Ann? She may be strong and willful, but she was also kind and gentle and someone he was certain tried to stay on the right side of the law.

What would she have done if he hadn't reached her in time at the convenience store or the hospital? A shudder ran down his spine, and he jerked against it. That in turn caused a snake of pain to run through his ribs, reminding him of the injury from the day before and to take things a little slower.

And on the thought of going slower, what had possessed him to kiss Ann? That was probably the last thing he should have done right now. When he'd pulled back, he had seen his confusion mirrored on her face. Why had he clouded up the situation by potentially veering them in a different direction? They needed to focus on survival, not building a relationship. He had no business starting something with her now. Not when she was vulnerable. Certainly not while he had Ginny to raise.

It's just that she had looked so beautiful. Appreciative. Vulnerable. And yes, trusting. He liked that, especially since it seemed to be what he struggled with most. He had not trusted her at first. He scowled at the thought. Trust was an issue from his past. He needed to move beyond that. Stop reliving the past, and instead, live for the future.

The future? It had been a long time since he cared about a woman. He had pretty much removed himself from the dating scene because he could not imagine bringing a woman into their home. He didn't want to do that to Ginny and didn't think it would be fair to a wife.

He'd learned that from Amelia, a woman he had dated about four years ago. She was a teacher at Ginny's school at the time. They met during pet day. Logan accompanied Ginny to help her transport Rocky the hamster to school. He started dating Amelia the next week. After several months, he realized he cared more for her a great deal more than he wanted to admit to himself or anyone else. When he finally acknowledged what was blooming in his heart and admitted it to her, she pulled back. Turns out, she wanted a good time, not a ready-made family. Shortly thereafter, the school year ended and she announced she was moving back to Texas to be near her family. The next week, the hamster had escaped through a door that had been left open. They never saw it again. Logan had thought it a euphemistically perfect farewell for the pet, considering how it mirrored Amelia's departure. He and Ginny had gone back to being just them, no hamster, no girlfriend. And in quick order, things had been fine again.

He rubbed the side of his neck. Was it possible he had come to care about Ann a little too much? His heart skipped a beat, and he found himself frowning. Yes, it was more than possible. More than probable, too. He was rather certain this had entered the already-a-done-deal stage. In fact, given what was swirling in his mind about spending time with her, and laughing with her, and protecting her, he was rather certain his attention already focused on her as much as it ever had on Amelia.

So, what now?

His house phone rang. The caller ID read, 'Jonathan Tate.' He took a deep breath and accepted the call.

"Where the blazes have you been?" Tate barked. "Is this how my chief of security acts when a crisis hits? You disappear? Why have you been calling everyone else at this company but not the man you should be calling?"

"I've been a little busy dodging bullets and potential killers," he groused. "Were the police in touch with you?"

"Yes, and that's—"

"Then you have a good idea of what's been happening and why I might choose to *not* bring that kind of danger to LubeRoyal. Seems to me that was the best decision on my part." *Remain calm.*

A hesitation on the line. "Yes, fine." Tate's snarled delivery suggested it was anything but fine to him.

"Besides, the program I set up is working. The employees are a little squeamish and spooked—nothing I can do anything about, by the way—but as for our processes, all systems are restored and production has returned to normal. I hope our company flag is flying at half-mast this week in honor of Harry Putnam."

"Who? What are you talking about?" There was no mistaking the annoyance in Tate's voice.

"Harry Putnam. Our employee. The man killed in the explosion, remember?"

"Yes, yes. Of course, I remember."

"What about Webb? Have you checked on him?"

"Who?"

Logan closed his eyes and pinched the bridge of his nose. *Patience.* "Webb Hollis. The CRS rep who was shot. His situation is dire. He's a husband and a father. Have you gone to the hospital? Spoken to his wife? Sent flowers?" As he talked, his hand clutched the phone tighter than he intended. He had to concentrate on relaxing his grip and his annoyance before his fingers locked tight.

"Why would I do that? He's a consultant. He gets paid for his work. It's not like he was volunteering his time here." Tate went quiet for a moment. "Yes fine, I'll have my assistant send flowers to the hospital. We'll call it miscellaneous and charge it back to CRS. When this has blown over and I'm rightfully placed at the helm, we're severing our contract with those people."

Rightfully placed at the helm ... Logan let those words go and instead challenged him with "*Those* people?"

"CRS, and especially that Bromberg idiot. They've done nothing but make matters worse."

"What are you talking about? Ann McCarthy saved our hides with the news media. Webb also was doing an excellent job coordinating information from the field and feeding it to management so timely decisions could be made." Logan was baffled. Why was Tate acing so irrationally? How could he not see what CRS had done to help them?

Tate huffed. "Look, just get in here. You need to tell the police that Henry Pullman—"

"Harry Putnam."

"Whatever. You need to tell the police you've seen him acting suspiciously in the past. Maybe that his behavior has been erratic, and he's threatened you."

"What! Why would I do that? First off, it's not true. Second, I barely knew the man. He worked nightshift. At the few meetings we attended together, he seemed like a decent guy. Not at all what you described. Did Collier confirm Harry had been acting this way?"

"Doesn't matter. Collier is no longer with us."

Logan slammed his fist on his desk. *Count to ten.* He rubbed his neck again. "Since when? I just talked to him late morning. He's been instrumental in—"

"Fifteen minutes ago. I fired him."

"On what grounds?"

"Too uncooperative and disloyal to LubeRoyal."

"Disloyal to ..." Logan jerked forward in his seat as a thought struck. "You fired him because he wouldn't lie for you or besmirch Harry's name. Didn't you?"

"Does it matter?" Tate growled. "Insubordination. He's no longer here. Spare me your morality speeches. This is business. The shootings are beyond our control. They look like a madman is on the loose, and we were victims. But there was still an explosion here. On our property. We don't need our grumpy neighbors raising a ruckus about us. We especially don't need our clients worried about placing orders. I need you here to verify what I said about Pullman. It's a white lie. No harm, no foul. It won't hurt anyone."

"It will hurt Harry's reputation."

"He's dead! What part of dead don't you understand? Besides, do you have any idea what it will cost to settle-up with insurance for his wife? You need to put aside your Pollyanna ideals and get your butt in here and be a team player."

Logan remained quiet, drumming his fingers on his desk. How he loathed the evil in this man! Would Tate truly force him to lie and besmirch Harry Putnam's character, in order to keep Ginny? Before he could figure out what to say, Tate continued.

"Remember, our agreement is not up yet. There's no way I'm turning over custody of my niece to a man who hasn't even learned what it takes to work a normal job and all the demands and responsibilities that come with it. Your responsibility is to come in here now, talk to the police, and clear us of this mess."

Logan's phone indicated another call coming in. *Thank you, Lord.* "Jonathan, I'm getting a call from Ginny's school. I'm sure you'll agree she is a priority to us both. I'll call you later."

Logan heard Tate yell, "Don't you dare hang—" before clicking off the call.

He punched into the call from the school, and his world spun from bad to worse.

Ginny was missing.

CHAPTER NINE

here are they?

Ann stood at the expansive window in the front of the cabin, staring down the long, winding lane that climbed the slope of the mountainside to the cozy home she had grown to love. The late afternoon sun shone through the uncurtained windows, punctuating the kitchen and dining areas with varied clusters of dappled light.

The valley beyond the lane looked peaceful, quiet, as the mid-afternoon sun cast dwarfed shadows to every bump and tree on the terrain. She sighed. The peaceful scenery belied what dwelled in her mind, her heart.

She felt the rise of concern in her stomach, too. Checked her watch. Touched the window. Shifted her stance. Checked her watch again.

Logan had been gone twelve minutes.

When he had stormed into the kitchen eighteen minutes earlier and announced Ginny was missing, he looked equal parts frantic and furious. Moments before, she had finished her confusing conversation with Sam and was still trying to make sense of it.

"Missing?" she repeated, springing to her feet. "What do you mean missing?"

Logan raised his hands in a 'who knows' gesture. "The principal called. Said she's missing. As in disappeared."

"What about Mom? And Barrett? He was standing guard. How could Ginny just disappear?"

"I don't know any more than you do. It's not like her to play tricks or run away. I'm sure there's a mistake, but I've got to get down there."

"Here," she said, rounding the table, disconnecting the recording device, and thrusting his cell phone to him. "Go. Call me on the home line as soon as you learn something."

He rubbed his neck. "I can't leave you here alone, and I think it's too dangerous to take you along." He paced in an agitated manner, ran a hand over his head. "The school's in an open setting with tons of doors. I've called Don, but he can't get here for thirty minutes."

Anxiety reflected in his eyes, and it made Ann's gut roil to think she was delaying him from helping his sister. "Logan, I'm not helpless. Give me a pistol. I know how to use it. And you have the alarm system. I'll be fine for a half-hour."

He stopped in front of her, studying her face. "You sure?" That quickly, however, he changed his mind. "No, I can't do that. It's too risky right now."

"Yes, you *can* do it. You must. Now, go."

He took a deep breath, expanding his chest. "Don't open the doors for anyone you don't know. And keep watch." He turned and disappeared toward the living room as he talked but was back in seconds, holding a pistol. "It's loaded. Safety's on the—"

She eyed the gun. "I know where the safety is."

"Oh, right," he nodded. "Let me show you how to work the alarm."

Thirty seconds later, with the alarm lesson complete, he said, "I better get going." He leaned in and kissed her cheek as though it was the most natural thing he could have done. Ann wondered if he even realized he'd done it. It was then she felt it: a small thrill, as if his certitude, his courage, his fortitude had seeped into her core. This was the sort of man, she was certain, who believed in his own ability, took his beliefs with him wherever he went, and would not stop until he accomplished what he knew to be the right thing to do.

"Back as soon as possible," he assured her as he scooped up his car keys and left.

After she closed the door behind him, Ann set the alarm then moved to the window to watch him climb into a perfectly restored green Bronco and head down the hill.

She hadn't moved from the spot for the past twelve minutes.

She looked at her watch. Correction, thirteen.

A watched pot never boils. She frowned at the thought. It might be true, but all the logic in the world wasn't enough to move her from this window right now. *Please keep her safe. She's so young and innocent.*

Another four minutes passed before she saw Barrett's silver Volvo heading up the lane toward the cabin. She waited, expecting to see Logan's car following behind.

But it didn't.

What did that mean? Should she call Logan and tell him they were back? No, they had to have passed one another on the road. Then again, what if this was all a trick? Could the thug have pretended to be the principal on the phone to lure Logan into a trap? No, she better not call anyone before she spoke with Barrett.

When the car drew near the house, she moved to the alarm and disengaged it. She checked to make sure the pistol's safety was intact before tucking it into the back waistband of her jeans.

Opening the door, she stepped out onto the driveway and found ...

Nothing.

The vehicle was there, but there was no one in sight.

Where had they gone? She called out, "Barrett?"

Behind her sounded the soft crunch of a footstep as if on loose stones. Suddenly some sixth sense, needling in her gut, caused her body to stiffen.

"He couldn't make it," a voice said from behind her.

That voice! Cold chills raced down her spine.

"I'll take that, thank you very much," the voice continued with a mocking air, and Ann felt the pistol being drawn from her waist as she swung around to face the owner of the voice.

A man with greasy blond hair, a crooked, bruised nose, and the most threatening look she'd ever seen pointed the pistol at her and grinned. Their gazes met. The unmistakable menace in his stare drove terror deep into her soul.

In her next heartbeat, she realized he was holding a small roll of industrial duct tape in his free hand. It was then she remembered there had been no signal. No single long, followed by two short beeps to signal familiarity with the security routine.

"What do you want?" A knot had lodged in her throat making her voice raspy. She could taste fear in her mouth.

"We'll discuss that later. Time's too tight. That driveway doesn't exactly provide many quick ways out of here, does it?" He smiled, his gaze boring into her with a look of delight mixed with self-satisfaction as though the exit was a mere challenge, and he would prove his shrewdness and resourcefulness to her. When she offered no response, he snarled, "Turn around."

If Ann could have checked her watch, she would bet it only took him about twenty seconds to tape her hands. Her mind scrambled for ways to stall for time. Don wouldn't arrive for another ten minutes. But how could she stall when she couldn't even think clearly?

Unfortunately, it took him only another thirty seconds to open the trunk and half-lift, half-thrust her into it. Then, they were off, bouncing down the mountain.

Trapped. That's all her mind could register. *I'm trapped!*

As frightening as that thought was, her next one trumped it, escalating her panic to a new level: The guy let her see him! He wasn't hiding behind a wrapped bandage or mask this time, or covering her eyes, or keeping her facing away from him. He intended to kill her! That's why he didn't mind if she saw him. No doubt he was responsible for Ginny being missing at school. Had he hurt her? Killed her? Or had he somehow stored her away long enough to create a diversion?

Fear that he intended to kill her sent her pulse pounding like she had just run for miles. Her breathing turned into ragged little gasps for air.

Calm down. She needed to focus. Collect her wits. Figure a way out of this.

Then, a corollary thought wrestled with her determination to remain calm: *Hurry up!* Think fast.

She couldn't see a thing in the trunk. It was too dark, like she'd fallen into the throat of a savage animal.

A trunk! She was in a trunk. Hadn't she seen something about kidnapped victims getting attention from other cars by kicking out the rear lights?

Calm down. Wait a second or two. Your eyes will acclimate to the darkness.

She concentrated on the movement of the car, hoping to ascertain which way it was moving. Lying prone in the dark, feeling every jar and bump in the road didn't help with acclimation.

Finally, she determined she faced the wrong way. The taillights were behind her.

Okay, no worries. All she had to do was start identifying where to kick.

The thought fizzled as the car slowed down. She heard the pavement turn to gravel. In a few seconds, the crushed stones quieted to the softer sounds of a natural terrain. The car came to a stop. She heard the man get out of the car. Next, he opened the trunk and brutally yanked her from its depths.

They were in a wooded cove hidden by sloping hills. She jerked her head around in a panic, hoping to see someone. Anyone.

Nothing. Only trees and nature and a battered tan van.

He pushed her toward the waiting van.

"We're taking this. The police will be looking for a stolen silver Volvo, not a van." He chuckled. "Sometimes even my own genius impresses me."

With one hand holding her in place, he opened the van's back doors.

"Why are you doing this?" she asked, her voice sounding unfamiliar. She needed to keep him talking. Try to delay him. "I don't even know you. I've never done anything to you. Look, I have a dying mother who needs me. If it's money you want—"

"Shut up!" he snarled and backhanded her across the face. Her head jerked to the side under the force of the blow, and pain exploded across her cheek.

He reached into the back of the van and pulled out a plastic container and a cloth. "You don't know me, but you know my sister."

He unscrewed the lid from the container.

"Your ... your sister?"

"Tracy. At the coffee shop. In the building where you work. And yes, I want money. But I want more money than you could ever give me ... alive. Dead, on the other hand, you're worth a lot more." He quickly doused the cloth with liquid, grabbed her, and held it over her mouth. She tried to squirm from his stronghold, tried to shake her head so that she could find a pocket of air, but his grip was too firm.

She panicked. He was trying to knock her out! Would he kill her while she was in that state of unknowing? Her terror ramped up even more as realization struck that she had absolutely no idea what he was talking about. Her confusion and panic worked against her, causing her to suck in deep, gasping bursts of air.

Within seconds, everything went dark.

WHEN SHE LATER AWOKE—A few minutes? Hours? She couldn't check her watch because her wrists were taped behind her back—she found herself sitting on the cold, concrete floor of a warehouse. Stacked crates formed walls around her in every direction. Tape sealed her mouth, her feet were bound in front of her, and her hands were tethered to the pole behind her. Her cheek stung where the man had slapped her, and her neck hurt, making her wish she still wore the brace the hospital had given her.

How ridiculous, she scolded herself. What good does a brace do when one may be seconds from dying? Her heart gave a great leap at the thought, and she tried to calm the galloping pace by reasoning it out. She was alive.

But for how long?

The unanswered question prompted adrenaline to shoot through her veins. Her pulse raced.

What's more, she was so cold! With all this anxiety pumping through her, how could she be cold? But she was. Icy bone-deep cold.

The frigid cold of mortal fear.

She stretched and looked around as much as the tape would allow. If she could get this gag off, maybe she could yell for help. Unfortunately, there was nothing close enough to use as leverage to work the tape off her mouth. Would anyone hear her anyway?

She settled back into a slouch. She could do nothing, except wait.

And pray.

NOT FOR THE FIRST TIME, Logan eyed his sister in the rearview mirror. She hadn't stopped talking since they climbed into the car, rattling on and on about the afternoon's activities, the kids' enjoyment of Nana Delores' tribal dancing, and who in the world it could have been that played a trick on her by locking her in one of the art supply closets.

When Logan had arrived, he joined the others in the school wide search to find her. Barrett and Mrs. McCarthy were frantic. When the police arrived minutes after Logan, he asked Barrett to return home to load up on weaponry and ammo. If Ginny had been taken from the school and a search effort became imminent, he wanted to be ready. Barrett hadn't been happy about it, wanting to stay put until things were resolved, but Logan knew refocusing Barrett was the best thing for him at the moment.

As it turned out, a full-scale search-and-rescue had not been necessary. Ginny was found in a locked storage closet in an empty classroom. She said she remembered someone grabbing her from behind and putting a hand over her mouth. The voice said, "Shh, we're playing hide and seek and you get to hide first."

When quizzed for details, she had nothing else to offer. She hadn't seen who it was and said the voice hadn't even sounded like anyone's real voice. The next thing she remembered was waking up on the floor of the closet. When she heard her name, she responded immediately.

Logan was convinced that whoever grabbed her had used chloroform to knock her out. That's why she had not responded when people called her name. She hadn't heard the guy or realized the danger she was in.

But he was certain Delores McCarthy had realized. She and Barrett had been right around the corner from that classroom when Ginny entered. Ginny's teacher told her supplies were limited in their own classroom's closet and to find paints for her project in that one.

He looked at Mrs. McCarthy now. She wore the stress of the afternoon on her face. He knew she'd feel better once she got home, saw Ann, and laid down to rest.

He turned his Bronco onto the long driveway home and headed up the side of the mountain.

Within minutes, he pulled the vehicle beside the house, beeping the signal. Don's car was there, but Barrett's was not.

As Logan climbed from the car, Don came out of the house.

Logan looked at Don as Ginny and Mrs. McCarthy headed toward the house. "Where's Barrett?"

Don sent him a look then glanced back to watch the ladies enter and close the door behind them. "I have a better question," he said with raised eyebrows. "Where's Ann?"

Logan's heart skipped a beat. "What do you mean?"

"She's not in the house. I just searched the entire thing—" As he talked, his gaze shifted, and he stared down the lane. His eyes pulled together as if studying something in the distance. "Here comes the answer to *your* question now," he said and broke off in a sprint.

Logan turned to see Barrett staggering up the lane, his body arched as if in pain and one hand on the side of his head.

He raced to catch up with Don.

Together, with them flanking him and Barrett's arms over their shoulders, they helped him reach the house and positioned him on the sofa.

A HALF-HOUR later Logan watched the ambulance pull away with Barrett then stepped back into the house. In the interim, Don had stabilized Barrett and administered aid to a very distraught Mrs. McCarthy. Ginny had spent a full fifteen minutes crying about Ann's disappearance then decided the only way for her to be a brave soldier was to pray. So she had gone into her room to do just that.

Don entered the kitchen where Logan stood, heaping scoops of coffee into a coffeemaker like he was mad at it. "Whoa there," Don said, eyeing Logan's work. "Even to scale Mount Everest you don't need coffee that strong."

"What? Oh ... right." He scooped coffee back into the bag, spilled some, then threw his hands up in defeat.

Don motioned for Logan to move away from the coffee. As he cleaned the spill, he asked, "You called Detective Redding?"

"I updated him on everything, not that it does us one bit of good." Logan watched Don clean the mess.

Don paused to study him closely. "You okay?"

"Okay? No, I'm not okay. Ann's missing and my sister could have been hurt. Even killed. Ann might be ... dead by now." He swallowed to keep from choking on the words. "I have no leads, no motive, no idea who would want to do this." He paused to lower his voice. This wasn't Don's fault. "I checked everything. No signs of breaking or forced entry. She must have thought it was Barrett who drove up. The surveillance tape only shows Barrett's car and a guy clearly dodging any cameras. When he climbs from the car, he's stooped over, hiding his face. When he approaches Ann, his back is to the camera."

"You think she mistook the guy for Barrett? Or maybe she knew him? You can't close your mind to that potential."

"He shoved her in the trunk!"

"Still could be a ruse. Done to throw you off. I'm just saying to stay open-minded to all possibilities."

Logan swiped a hand back and forth over the lower half of his face. *What did all this mean, and who was behind it?*

"When I left to help Mrs. McCarthy," Don continued, "Barrett had started telling you what he remembered. None of that helped?"

"None." Logan shrugged "Well, just that the guy had blond hair and a crooked nose. That's something at least, but not enough to work with. He said the guy was walking near the entrance of the property. Barrett thought he probably wasn't a threat since he was on foot. He stopped to see what the guy was doing there. Next thing he knew, the guy had a gun on him and ordered him to get out of the car. The guy shot at the ground near Barrett's feet. The gun had a silencer on it, but it still startled Barrett. Took him off his guard, giving the guy the opportunity to belt him across the face with the gun. Then a few well placed kicks into the abdomen and another blow to the back of his head pretty much assured Barrett was down for a while."

"It's a good sign he didn't kill Barrett." Don leaned back against the counter and crossed his ankles.

"Sign of what?" Logan huffed, fisting his hands.

"That he's not just out to kill. He has a purpose. An intent. A target. We just need to figure out what it is and who he is." Don shifted his gaze to the floor before glancing back with a hardened look. "Look, I like Ann, too. A lot. She seems like a genuine and caring woman, and I hope she is. But what do we know about her past? You mentioned a former boyfriend. Maybe he's not as former as we think. You have to be open to all options."

"Maybe, but I don't think so." Logan explained the call they had placed together to Aiden. "He sounded anxious to prove his worth to her again, but he didn't sound desperate or willing to take stupid chances with his new freedom."

"You're certain she didn't have a change of heart? Maybe she called him back in private after that conversation."

"Not Ann. I've gotten to know her in the past few days. I've watched her. Heard her talking with her mom." His mind flashed back to the night before. He had been asleep on the couch for several hours when he heard someone move through the living room. Her aroma hit him. That herbal fragrance of hers. He opened his eyes to watch her step onto the veranda. He should have gotten up to tell Ann and her mother that it was best if they not go outside, even to the veranda, until the threats were eradicated. But what he heard had stifled his intent.

Ann's mother had said, "I like him." That immediately followed with Ann asking, "You like who?"

"Logan, of course. Your new boyfriend."

Ann's voice had gone higher when she responded. "He's not my boyfriend, Mama."

Logan had heard an edge of amusement in Delores's tone when she followed that with, "We'll see. You like him, too. I can tell."

"What? Mama, don't go there. And don't give me that look. Okay, you're right, yes, I like him. What's not to like? He's caring, intelligent, successful, brave—"

"Don't forget easy on the eyes."

"Mother!"

"Well, he is. And he's very different from the men you've dated in the past. Much better than Aiden."

Ann had sniggered. "A Saint Bernard would be better than Aiden. At least I'm safe with Logan—" She had broken off with a groan. "Listen to me. Now you've got me thinking along those lines. Logan is a good guy, but we both have our own lives. It's this situation that brought us together. Nothing more."

"We'll see. Stranger things have brought people together. Never underestimate God's ability."

"We'll see nothing. Come on, Mama. It's time you went to bed and got some rest."

"So, now what?" Don's baritone voice interrupted Logan's thoughts, bringing him back to the moment.

Logan huffed, trying to refocus and release pent-up anxiety. "The police are scouting the area to see if they can find Barrett's car. The thing is, it's rural around here, and I doubt the guy is a local. He must have had another car parked somewhere."

"If he's been surveilling you, he could have figured out Ginny was at the school. But how could he know Barrett would come back here prior to the rest of you?"

Logan thrust a hand over the top of his head. "Who knows? Maybe he made a good guess. Maybe there's more than one person involved."

"That's true. There could be an elaborate network of demented people mixed in all this."

"Or maybe the guy stood on any of the hills around here and watched Barrett pull away from the school," Logan reasoned. "This terrain can provide some perfect security for some things but also add a layer of risk in another."

"Well, you're right that it doesn't sound like a predator grabbing

Ann at random. It's been too intentional all along. But I don't see what you can do right now except leave this in the hands of the police."

Logan shook his head and averted his gaze as he paced away from Don. "You're right. I know the police are on it. But this inactivity is driving me insane." He stopped and placed a hand over his abdomen. It wasn't his abs hurting this time but rather a twisted lump he felt in his gut. *Anxiety. Dread. Pure anger.*

"You're not inactive. You're thinking. Brainstorming. Keeping an open mind to all possibilities. That *is* doing something."

At Don's words, Logan swung around to stare at his friend. A sarcastic syllable of a sound escaped his lips. How apropos of Don to mention the word *possibilities*. "The problem is, I always seem to be content dealing in probabilities. Not possibilities." He swallowed before continuing. "Ann and I have talked about that."

Don hesitated. Logan watched his friend studying him with skeptical eyes. Finally, with a nod, Don said, "I understand."

Logan turned away again, moving around the room erratically. "Then again, I should have called Ann from the school. There was opportunity after we found Ginny. I kept meaning to, but the time went by so quickly. I figured Ann was busy making calls, too. I thought she might be on the phone with Bromberg. I didn't want to interrupt that. She knew that call was essential."

"Her business partner? The one not injured?"

"That's him. When I heard about Ginny being missing, all I could focus on was getting to that school. I didn't even ask if she'd called him yet. I was going to listen to their conversation afterward ..." Logan stopped in his tracks, jerking his gaze to the table. The recording device! It still sat where Ann had left it when she disconnected his phone to hand it to him.

He hustled to the recorder. *Please let it give me something to work with.*

CHAPTER TEN

L ogan slammed his Bronco into park, turned off the engine, and bounded from the vehicle. Time was of the essence. He sprinted up the front steps of Sam Bromberg's massive house and pounded his fist on the oak door.

After listening to the voice recording between Ann and Bromberg, he and Don and had made plans. Next, Logan secured Bromberg's address from Claire at CRS, and broke every speed limit he passed to get to Bromberg's estate in Potomac, Maryland. Don had promised to remain available at the house should Ginny or Mrs. McCarthy need him.

Logan had prayed the entire trip, too. And hoped. Hoped he wasn't running down a rabbit hole. Hoped the early evening rush-hour traffic would cut him a break. Hoped he was driving closer to a resolution, not farther from it. Particularly, hoped his efforts would help Ann regardless of how shot-in-the-dark his hunches were.

He pounded the door again, yelling, "Bromberg, open up!" Then, he took his anger out on the doorbell, determined to push it until it either broke or someone answered.

The door moved when an anxious-looking Sam appeared, inching it open less than a foot. He wore jeans and an unkempt shirt. His hair was mussed, like he had run a hand through it too many times that day. "Kassell! What are you doing here?" He hissed, standing partially behind the door as if he might want to slam it shut on a whim.

Without hesitation, Logan shoved the solid wood door open and would have barreled into Sam had the guy not stepped out of the way. The marbled foyer was huge and smelled stale. Logan's voice echoed as he said, "We need to talk. *Now*."

With an exaggerated sigh and a pout, Bromberg shut the door and gestured him into a sitting room off to the right. "I can't believe Ann told you where I live."

"She didn't. Claire did."

He cursed. "I'll fire her. She knows better than to—"

"You'd be a fool to fire her. She wouldn't give me your house address ..." He swirled his gaze around the room, a look of disgust on his face, "or should I say *mansion* address until I told her Ann has been kidnapped."

Sam's eyes grew wide, and he reached out to steady himself by placing a hand on a wingback chair. "Kidnapped? What are you talking about? I just spoke with her a few hours ago." His eyes pulled together and he stiffened his spine. "Is this some kind of trick?"

"I know about your conversation with Ann today. Every detail. Why would you think I'm trying to trick you? Feeling guilty about something?" Logan fisted his hands.

Fear flickered in Sam's eyes. "I don't know what she told you, but she seemed hysterical when we talked. I can imagine how she misunderstood everything I said. Probably enhanced it."

Logan tilted his head. *Did his disgust show?* "She didn't tell me anything. I heard it all on tape."

Sam's head jerked back. "That's illegal. You had no right. I could take this to court—"

"Yeah, you do that. You want to sue *before* or *after* I play the tape for the police and your family, implicating you in this mess? Sabotage, second-degree murder, aggravated assault, kidnapping. Don't forget general greed and stupidity ... your rap sheet keeps getting longer and longer."

"I didn't do those things!" he blubbered, looking panicky. His hand shook as he swiped it over his head.

"At a minimum, you were an accomplice."

Sam's eyes grew wide, and he pulsed his palms at Logan. "Okay, okay, slow down. No court. We'll call it a stalemate."

Logan stepped forward and grabbed Sam by the shirt lapels, yanking him close. "There will be no slowing down until we find Ann. If she's harmed in anyway, I personally will hold you responsible. You got it?"

Eyes wide, Sam bobbed his head with exaggerated movements and spread his hands wide at his side as if in supplication. He lowered his voice. "Alright, I get it. What do you want from me?"

Logan didn't want to let go of him, but he did. Still to appease himself, he wasn't exactly gentle about it, causing Sam to stagger back a step to gain balance. "Tracy. You said she told her brother about you two. What are their full names? Any spouses? Where will I find them?"

"We're home!" A voice called from a distant corner of the house as though someone had entered through a back door.

"Shhh," Sam looked toward the door leading into the room. "That's my wife and kids. It's after five-thirty for Pete's sake. There's no need to—"

Logan grabbed his arm, securing a firm hold. "Are you hearing me?" He snarled the words but kept his voice low. "I don't care about your wife or you or your affairs or your little get-rich-quick schemes. Your partner is in the hospital fighting for his life, and Ann might be next ... if she's even lucky enough to still be alive. I don't know how you live with yourself. Right now, you're facing a long haul in prison to work on it. So, yell to your wife that you're with an associate then start talking."

Sam jerked his arm free and stepped back a few paces. Dutifully, he called out to his wife as Logan had instructed then shut the French doors that led into the sitting room. "Her name is Tracy Harrell. She was married once. Her brother is George Clemens. He's never been married, and as far as I know, has no significant other."

"Where will I find him?"

"I don't know. I've never met the guy."

Logan fisted his hands again and stepped toward Sam. Sam backed up farther and showed his palms again. "It's true! Look ..." he hesitated long enough to gaze toward the sitting room door again. Lowering his voice, he continued, "Tracy and I may have had our little fling, but I wasn't involved in her life to that extent. She's uneducated. Trashy. Rough around the edges, if you know what I mean." He shrugged. "A good time, that's all."

Logan pulled his shoulders back and studied Sam. "You disgust me."

Sam muttered a sound of annoyance. "Spare me your righteousness and your hypocrisy. I know you work closely with Tate, and he's as sleazy as they come. I don't care whether you approve of me or not." He paused, took a deep breath, and shook his head, almost looking contrite. "But I do care about Ann. I had no idea Tracy was pulling her brother into some harebrained scheme. I get the impression he's a little slow up here." Sam tapped a finger against his head. "Tracy means everything to him. She's the one to talk to. I'm innocent in Ann's disappearance. You gotta believe me. I had nothing to do with it!"

Logan couldn't believe the audacity of this man. "We'll discuss where Tracy got the idea for this later. Right now, I need to figure out where to find Clemens. Start taxing your memory because if I don't find her in time, I'm going to make sure the police take you down. It will be a long time before you sleep in this mansion again."

Sam staggered around to the front of the wingback chair he'd been protectively squirreling behind and dropped with a thud as though bracing himself for the uncomfortable conversation ahead.

ANN FELT a pain shoot through her back and legs. Bound and gagged and sitting on a cold concrete floor for hours wasn't her idea of comfort. Then again, she was still alive.

But for how long?

How long had she been here? The only illumination in the place came from narrow horizontal windows that hung about a foot from the top of the two-and-a-half story warehouse. The light had grown significantly darker while she was there. What would happen when there was no light left at all? Would she be in complete darkness? For how long? Would mice and rats and other little creatures start scurrying around her? The thought sent chills down her spine.

She thought about Ginny and the fear she may be suffering. The girl was such an innocent in all this. *Please let her still be alive.* Logan would never forgive himself if anything happened to his little sister.

Her thoughts flowed to her mother. Sweet, trusting Delores McCarthy. Would she ever get over losing her daughter, because right now it seemed imminent?

Hold it together, Ann!

Something one of her elementary teachers had said came to mind. Mrs. Benson had taught her class that F-E-A-R stood for False Evidence Appearing Real.

But this fear was the real kind, wasn't it? The duct tape, this building, these crates, blond guy—all too real.

False Evidence Appearing Real.

Despite the angst, a peace entered Ann's core. Her teacher was right: Outlook helps determine outcome. Webb and Tia had helped her see that, too. She needed to focus on the here and now.

She concentrated on calming her heartbeat and her breathing. *In. Out. Slow it down.*

A sound came from off to her right. A door! She heard it shut then footsteps moved toward her. Within seconds a blond guy hovered over her.

Tall. Muscular build. Ratty, bleached jeans. Green shirt. Grayish blue eyes. Crooked nose. Pointy chin guy hovered. Button-down. She tried to absorb it all. Faith and positive thinking dictated she might have the opportunity to identify him in a line-up, didn't it?

He reached down and yanked the tape from her mouth, causing a momentary streak of pain to her skin. "You're in luck. At least for now," he chuckled. "Can't take you out until it's dark. If I killed you now, I'd have to drag you out. That would be even more suspicious." He paused, glancing toward the outer wall. "Bunch of idiot druggies hanging outside. One of 'em might be sober enough to remember me bringing you outta' here. But I heard 'em talking. They'll be gone soon. Off for another hit."

He pulled a crate close and dropped on it to face her. As he positioned himself, he reached for his knee, a reminder to Ann that he had hurt it in the hospital stairwell. "Can't believe how stupid kids are these days. Doing drugs. What a way to ruin your life."

Whereas kidnapping and murder aren't avenues for ruining one's life?

She didn't ask it out loud. Why take the chance of provoking him? Besides, she didn't want the confirmation that her death was impending although he'd as much as assured her of it. The truth was inescapable.

He seemed to consider himself quite smart, but his mannerisms and slow verbal delivery suggested otherwise. Besides, didn't all thieves and murderers think they were clever and above the law? Maybe if she got him to discuss his scheme, she could talk her way to freedom. Or at least buy some time. But first she had to know the damage he'd already done. In a raspy voice she asked, "Did you ... did you kill Ginny?"

He grinned, and it verged on the diabolical. A predator's grin. She noticed for the first time he hadn't spent much of his life in a dentist chair. "The kid? Nah, I wouldn't hurt a kid. They'll find her on the floor in one of the school closets. That maneuver worked out rather well. I'm proud of that one."

"What about Barrett?"

"Who?"

"Owner of the silver Volvo. You drove his car to the house."

"Oh, him." He waved it away. "Big dude. Nah, he'll live, too. Probably enjoy a vacation in a comfy hospital for a while, but he'll recover."

"You did all that to create a diversion. To approach the house when no one else was around. Why? I at least want to know that. You've killed the LubeRoyal employee. Shot Webb. Now you've taken me. Why?"

He looked affronted. "I didn't have anything to do with that sloppy explosion at LubeRoyal. I wouldn't kill without good cause. They can't pin that on me. But I had a suspicion it was going to occur, so I took advantage of the timing. Soon as Tracy called and told me about the explosion, I knew I had my chance. Knew the timing couldn't be better. Smart, eh? Your disappearance will be blamed on the idiot that caused the explosion."

Confused, Ann pressed for understanding. "So, you didn't cause the explosion ... or put that fake bomb casing in my bag? Then who did?"

"Explosive? Not my thing. Too messy. Too much work. Too danger-ous. You'll have to ask Sam or that Tate guy about that one." He hesi-tated and clicked his fingers together. "Oh wait, you won't be able to. You'll be dead." He chuckled as though titillated by his own cleverness. The hairs on her neck rose. She prayed her sudden spurt of fear didn't show. With new urgency, escaping overcame her desire to know why this was happening to her. She needed to get her hands and feet free. Somehow.

"I ... I need to use the restroom. Surely you can extend me that one dignity?"

He scowled. "Yeah, all right. Why not? It's going to be almost an hour or two before we can leave here anyway."

He removed a knife from his back pocket and leaned over to cut the tape at her feet. "There's a john in the back. No windows. I knew this place would be perfect. Secluded. No one ever comes here anymore." He was behind her now, and she heard the tape rip as he cut it. Within seconds her hands and feet were free. She massaged her wrists where the tape had rubbed them.

"Well? Get up," he growled.

She tried, but complying wasn't all that easy. Her legs were cramped, so she couldn't climb to her feet in a smooth effort. Instead, she got one knee beneath her, pressed her hands to the floor, and pushed up.

He made an impatient noise then leaned in, grabbed her arm, and yanked her up. He was so close, Ann could smell his tobacco breath, see the faint stubble on his chin and a tiny scar near his lower lip. He shoved her forward. "That way."

Think Ann. Look around. Find a weapon!

She moved as slowly as she could. *Buy some time!* Her feet inched along, but her heart was on overdrive and cold sweat poured from her body. They'd gone several yards before he shoved her from behind. "Get going. Move faster."

Her legs were still numb from the way she'd been sitting so his push caused her to lose her footing, and she fell. She braced with her hands to keep her face from smacking into the floor. In the next moment, she sprawled on her stomach.

With her head inches from the floor, she saw a glint under a raised pallet of crates beside her. The fading sun still cast enough light through the upper windows that it appeared shiner than anything around it. In that split second, she focused, taking in its shape. Long and narrow. Best of all, it was pointy and sharp. *A box cutter!*

Her shaking hand reached for it as blond guy bent over to pull her to her feet. Her fingers closed around it so snug the edges cut into her palm. Her heart thrummed loudly.

She had to do this. *Now!* Before he discovered it in her hand.

His sausage fingers yanked her up a second time. Spurred by terror, she clenched her teeth and swung around, slamming the cutting edge into the side of his neck with all her strength. She shuddered for a heartbeat at the feel of it sinking into his flesh.

He bellowed and staggered sideways, reaching for the cutter. She screamed too, yanked her arm from his hold, and shoved him. As he dropped to one knee, she turned and careened in the opposite direction.

"Help!" She screamed repeatedly until her lungs ached. She ran fast, her feet barely touching the floor, her legs pumping voraciously thanks to newfound adrenaline. Around one stack of crates then another. Always heading toward an exterior wall. Her heart thundered. Where was a door?

She faltered, scanning the wall, searching for an exit. Her hesitation fueled new fear because she could hear his curses, his clodding footsteps barreling toward her, closing in quickly. He was going to catch her ...

Hurry, hurry, hurry!

Around another stack of crates then a pile of empty boxes of mismatched sizes, and there it was. A door! Not an exterior door. But still a door. She dashed to it and fumbled with the knob. *What was the matter with it? Calm down, Ann, it's you, not the knob.*

Come on, come on!

She risked a petrified glance over her shoulder and saw him a few yards behind her. His face was contorted with fury and his neck covered in blood. His sore knee barely slowed him a bit. She shrieked again, this time a wail of anguish.

He was so close! She hadn't realized how close he was because she'd only heard her own labored breathing for the past several heartbeats.

With one more twist of the knob and a thrust, she wrenched the door open and raced through.

Too quickly, walls closed in on her. The room was warm, the air stale. It was an interior room with only one exit—the one she'd used to enter!

Worse still, a dim rectangle of light poured through the open door, silhouetting a bound and startled Aiden tethered to a straight-back chair on the opposite side. He had a gash on his forehead, a split lip, and a purplish eye, covered with a sagging eyelid as though muscle control had been compromised.

Behind, blond guy followed her through the doorway, his eyes blazing like the devil.

Faced with the inevitable, she hunched in terrified expectation as he grabbed her shoulders with a curse, twisted her around, and quick as a snake, backhanded her, one slug across both her cheek and lips that dropped her to her knees. A hard shock stilled her and she tensed, expecting more.

She thought she heard Aiden yell at blond man. Something about there being no need to hurt her. Blond guy responded for him to shut up, followed by a comment about Aiden now having to die because of her.

A taste of metallic blood assailed her. She put her hands on the floor to push up, but blond guy followed the abuse with a kick to her ribs.

A loud whoosh exited her lungs, and pain exploded through her core, expanding outward in an instant. She would have screamed but the burning irritation didn't allow it. Instead, she writhed, gasping for air. Tears stung her eyes. Trickled onto her skin.

Blond guy grabbed another straight-back chair, slamming it tight against the back of Aiden's. He grabbed a chunk of Ann's hair and wrenched her to her feet again. Dizziness seized her, and a shaft of pain shot down her neck. Next, he manhandled her into the chair then removed a bandana from his back pocket and tied it around the gouge in his neck. Finally, he taped her feet and hands together.

As he tethered her to the chair with rough thrusts, he took pleasure in describing how much he was going to enjoy killing her. "So slowly," he concluded, "you'll wish you'd never been born."

Logan stood in the shadows around a corner from Apartment 4B in a lackluster building in southeast D.C. The hallway was narrow and smelled of mold and a mixture of fried foods and pungent foreign spices, as though a month's worth of meals had never been vented out of the building. He'd been waiting in that shabby spot for fifteen minutes. Claire and Bromberg had both confirmed Tracy closed her coffee shop at about 6 p.m.

When Logan left Bromberg's place, he knew it was too late to reach the CRS building to confront her at the shop. Instead, with the address Bromberg had given him, he headed straight to her apartment, hoping and praying she would go directly home after work.

He heard feet padding toward the apartment door. Then, the sounds of a key being inserted and a door opening. He hurried around the corner.

"Ms. Harrell," he said, his voice firm, authoritative. He moved into her personal space, looming over her.

She looked up, startled. When their gazes met, a look of fear crossed her heavily painted and foundationed face, convincing Logan that Bromberg hadn't called Tracy to give her a heads-up. The guy had seemed genuinely concerned about getting Ann back safely. What's more, Logan had threatened to expose Sam to his wife if he forewarned Tracy.

"How do you know who I am?" Her words came out rushed, her stare and tone both reeking of disdain for him. "Just go away. I have nothing to say to you." She fidgeted with the bag draped from her shoulder and hurried through the door, attempting to thrust it shut behind her.

Logan stuck his foot in the door's path and placed a stopping palm at shoulder height. For a moment, they struggled with the direction the door would go. Logan easily won, and he pushed his way in, shutting the door behind him. "I'm not going to hurt you. I want some answers. If you don't give them, then I'll get the police here in nanoseconds and they can ask them."

She backed away from him and tossed her purse on the couch. "You're that guy I saw at CRS the other day."

"That's right. You were quite chummy with Sam Bromberg that morning."

"Yeah? So what? Nothing illegal about that."

"No, what you two do is your own business. But what you do to my company and to my friends is another matter. Ann McCarthy has been kidnapped, and I have reason to believe you know all about it. I also suspect you might be involved in it."

She shook her head in wild movements. "I didn't have anything to do with that explosion at LubeRoyal if that's what you're talking about. That was Sam and Jonathan Tate's doing."

Logan jerked his shoulders back. He hadn't anticipated that bit of news.

Then again, could he believe her? It didn't matter. To figure out who instigated and carried out the explosion would be a waste of time. *For now.* That could be investigated later.

All he needed now was to find Ann. He'd learned enough interrogation in Afghanistan to know that when people are accused of something, they often spill information on someone to point the finger elsewhere. Fine then. He needed some finger-pointing right now. Needed some leads. He rubbed his chin.

"That's interesting. Because Bromberg says it was your doing. The explosion, the dead employee, the kidnapping attempts." A lie, but necessary to throw her off track.

A look of panic etched lines on her face. "That's not true! I had nothing to do with that." She choked on a sob. "Sam wouldn't say that …"

"He said you had delusional plans about the two of you getting together. He also claims you pulled your brother in on this. Either you or your brother have kidnapped Ann, and I want to know where she is."

"I didn't have anything to do with Hollis or Ann being hurt." She began to shake so badly Logan thought she might fall over. With another sob, she dropped onto the couch. "It was my brother, George. He's a little ... slow. Off in the head. He got in a brawl at work and lost his job. Got desperate for money. When I mentioned I wanted to get back together with Sam, he saw it as our ticket to financial freedom. He's very protective of me." She talked slowly, sniffling as she continued. "Sam once told me CRS was a three-way partnership. George figured with a partner or two out of the way, CRS would be worth more to Sam." She yanked a tissue from a box on the coffee table. "And therefore, to me. For our future."

Delusional, Logan thought. "Where will I find your brother?"

"I don't know." She made a hand gesture of defeat. "He lost his apartment, so he's been living in a van."

"What does it look like?"

"Tan. A Chevrolet, I think."

"When do you expect to see him next?"

"Your guess is as good as mine." She blew her nose. "He only stops here every two or three nights to shower."

Logan began to pace. He didn't have anything to work with. He doubted her story, but he had no proof and didn't know which parts were truth and which lies. She hadn't provided any direction for him to go.

He stopped pacing at her entertainment console when something caught his gaze. On the shelves to the right were several personal photographs. One featured Tracy with a man. "Is that him? Is that George?"

She glanced over. "That's him."

Logan looked closer. The background looked like a bad part of D.C. The southeast Anacostia quadrant. "Where was this taken?"

"Anacostia riverfront. Old warehouse area. It's where George worked. Said he liked it because they were his kind of people, and the cops didn't go there much."

As Logan took out his cell phone and snapped a picture of the framed photograph, a knock sounded at the door, followed by a deep voice yelling, "Police. Open up."

Tracy's gaze darted to meet Logan's. "You called the police?" Her words hovered harshly in the thick discomfort of the air between them.

"That's right. About twenty minutes ago." He picked up the photo, moved to the door, and opened it.

Two officers stood at the door, erect and poised to deal with whatever awaited them. The taller of the two checked a notepad in his hand. "You Logan Kassell?"

"I am." He pulled out his license and showed it to them. "You talked to Detective Redding?"

"Affirmative. I'm Officer Semansky. This is Officer Calhoun. We're here to escort ..." He checked his notes again, "Tracy Harrell to the station for questioning."

Logan stood back and gestured toward her. "She's all yours." He handed the photograph to Officer Semansky. "This is the guy Redding is after. Now if you'll excuse me, I have urgent matters to attend to."

CHAPTER ELEVEN

For the past dozen years, the Anacostia Riverfront area—known for its high crime rate and drug activities—reputedly bore the worrisome distinction as home to at least a third of all homicides in Washington D.C. The warehouse portion wasn't large, and there were at least a dozen buildings, most of them abandoned and left to fall into disrepair. What's more, the sun was setting, making it challenging to spot a tan van. Despite the clear evening sky, Logan doubted moonlight would be able to effectively spill past the tall buildings to flood the streets below.

He sighed, pondering the task ahead. At this point, he would be happy if finding a tan van were the least of his concerns. The guy could have ditched it for a different vehicle by now, or headed out in any number of directions. *He could have taken Ann anywhere ...*

He checked the time on his cell phone. Twenty-five minutes since he had left Tracy's apartment. Ten since he spoke to Detective Redding and forwarded the picture of George Clemens. The detective had spent twice as much time lecturing him about staying out of police work as explaining his coordination and reciprocity efforts with the District police.

Logan respectfully agreed Redding's advice was sound but ignored it anyway. Before clicking off the call, he said, "I understand, but I'll still see the police there."

Ann was in dire danger. There was no way he was going to stay out of it. Plus, it was always good procedure to let law authorities know when you, as a civilian, would be at a target area.

He slowed to a crawl, assessing the riverfront and determining his approach. Finally, alley by alley, he scoured, lights off, driving slowly up one then down another. There was more litter and questionable characters on the streets than there were vehicles with four wheels intact.

What if Clemens was using a new vehicle? Could he have pulled accomplices with other transportation into his scheme, just as he'd tried to do with Aiden Rutherford? If so, how well-armed would they be?

Logan pounded his fist against the steering wheel. He had so little to work with! Thoughts of Ann filled his mind. He never should have left her alone. He could have taken her to the school with him. He should have known Ginny's disappearance was a deception, as fake as the bomb Ann pulled from her bag the other morning. If anything happened to her ...

He gripped the wheel like he wanted to extract blood from it. When had she taken up so much room in his heart? Would he ever get the chance to tell her how he felt? *Please, she just came into my life, into my care. Keep her safe. She doesn't deserve this. Her mother needs her. Let her live. Let me have more time with her.*

He turned another corner then another before he saw it. A battered tan van! Up ahead, at the end of the passageway. He stopped and backed his Bronco out of the narrow alley, staying in reverse until he was about half way down a perpendicular block. Before he left Smithsburg, he had packed two pistols. He grabbed them now and exited through the passenger door, keeping away from the main road. Once on his feet, he tucked one of the pistols in the back waistband of his jeans. The other, he kept at the ready.

He hustled to the corner, turned into the alley where he'd seen the van, and sidled up to the wall of the brick warehouse. Moving through the shadows, he hugged the building to his back as he inched along.

After progressing a few yards, he spotted a man emerging from the door nearest to the waiting van. Logan was too far away to confirm the guy was Clemens, but his size and blond hair fit the man in Tracy Harrell's picture. Plus, the guy seemed to favor his right leg. Could be due to the injury sustained on the hospital stairwell. Logan's gut told him this was Clemens.

The guy climbed in the van and drove away from the building, heading down the alley toward him. Logan shrank into the nearest doorframe. Thankfully, it was hidden by an array of garbage dumpsters. He crouched down as the van sped by.

It was too dark to see the driver well, but Logan could tell he drove one-handed, holding something at his neck with the other hand. He read the departing license plate.

Could Ann be inside the warehouse? In the van? Decision time. Follow the van or search the building?

He called Detective Redding. "I think Clemens just left an Anacostia warehouse. Red brick, fronting the river. Four roads from Martin Luther King Jr. Avenue. I'm going in. He took off in a tan van. D.C. license." Logan rattled off the plate's number then clicked off the call, giving an angry Redding no chance to rebut.

He hurried to the double doors through which Clemens had exited. One pull and he was in.

Once inside he found himself in a stairwell. Time to choose. Climb the steps to other floors or start searching the first floor.

Clemens would want ease of access and egress. Logan chose the first floor. May as well start there and work his way up if he had to. He pushed through a set of double doors, entering a passage wrapping to the right. He followed until it ended into a massive storage area filled with lengthy rows of crates stacked one on top the other. Four steps ahead to his left was a door marked "Restroom." He eased it open and found a light switch. A toilet, urinal, and sink but otherwise empty.

He flipped off the light, eased the door shut, and inched forward about a yard.

His back to the wall, he froze and held his breath, listening. A moment ticked by. Then two. He couldn't be sure but he thought he heard muffled voices filtering from somewhere in the back.

A conversation meant at least two people. What's more, Clemens could return at any time.

He hoped the police hurried.

"YOU OKAY?" Aiden's voice sounded from behind Ann. They were sitting back to back, their hands and feet bound, chairs tethered together. When blond guy stormed from the room, he hadn't even bothered to shut the door behind him.

No, I'm not okay! I'm tied against my will to my old boyfriend in a smelly old warehouse waiting for a lunatic to come back and kill me! How well could I be?

"About the same as you, I imagine," Ann said. "Is he the reason for the damage to your face?"

"Yeah. Caught me as soon as I stepped into the warehouse."

Ann paused a moment. Her instinct was to say, 'What were you thinking?' but the truth is she was grateful to not be alone. Even if her only companion was someone who had once tried to break her. "How did you know to come here?"

"He's the guy that came to the boarding house. When he left, I looked out the window and saw his van. It's kinda distinctive with its dents and scrapes. So, when Sam told me you were in Smithsburg—"

"Sam told you?" *He must have gotten the address from Tate.*

"I told you I was going to call him. Was he always that terse? Anyway, I knew the town wasn't very big. And there is only one large mountain near it. I wanted to talk to you in person. Not through someone else's phone. So, I drove to Smithsburg and started looking around. Next thing I know, I see that familiar-looking van pull out of a dense grove of trees. The van and the location ... obviously, it seemed suspicious, so I followed."

Ann startled. "Just like that? No plan in mind. No reason to suspect the guy had even done anything. What did you think you would do once he stopped?"

"I don't know. Keep following. Wherever he went. Find out where he lived. What he was up to. The guy seemed intent on getting to you.

It bothered me." Aiden grew quiet for a couple seconds before continuing. "I love you, Ann. I didn't want anything to happen to you."

Ann felt nothing but sadness at his words. "That's nice, Aiden. I appreciate it. But now instead of just me dying," she said, her voice matching her misery, "it looks like you will as well."

He emitted an exasperated sound. "I got that impression. I hadn't seen his face prior to you racing into the room. Right after he hit you, he said now that I've seen him, I would have to die."

Ann flinched. "Sorry."

"Hey, not your fault. I'm the one that wanted to be a hero in your eyes. Who is this guy anyway? What does he want from you?"

"I'm not sure. He's the brother of a woman who works in the coffee shop in my office building. Tracy's her name. Apparently, she fancies herself in love with Sam." She thought of Logan's comment that he had seen the two share an impassioned moment. She should have paid it more heed. Should have given more credence to Logan's suspicions of Sam. "Tracy thinks Sam is worth lots of money and that he'll leave his wife to be with her. I guess this guy, the brother, thinks that with me and Webb gone, Sam will have more money to be with her."

Aiden whistled a sound of incredulity under his breath. A few seconds of silence descended before he spoke, his voice taking on a wistful tone. "It's always about money, isn't it? Crime, I mean. Money or broken hearts."

Was he speaking personally or generally? "I suppose."

"I imagine he's gone only long enough to do something about that nasty gash on his neck. You did that?" Without waiting for her answer, he continued. "When he comes back ..." His voice trailed off.

She wondered how Aiden would have finished that sentence. When blond guy comes back, then what? They would die? They could overpower him? Fat chance of that, considering they were bound and the man was free. He was also angry, carried weapons, and injured because of her. Aiden had to be as scared as she was. The best thing she could do was keep him focused on their logistics and potential escape, however hopeless it seemed at the moment. *Outlook helps determine outcome.* "Maybe the guy's off his game. Getting sloppy. He didn't gag us. He hadn't gagged you at all. I wonder why?"

She felt Aiden shift as though annoyed by a question that, to him, must seem ill-placed and ill-timed.

"I don't know," he said in an exasperated voice. "I guess he had no more cloth."

"He could have used the tape."

"What does it matter now?" Aiden's voice revealed withering patience. He sighed, his tone softening when he spoke again. "When he hauled me in here, he said this room was sound-proof. I guess that's why he didn't bother."

"Sound-proof? In a warehouse?"

"Not that unusual. This way, business can go on even as noisy skid-loaders and trucks work in the storage area."

"But now the door's open."

"Which means he's coming back very soon and knows no one will hear us if we yell." He cleared his throat. "Look Ann, if we only have a few minutes to live, I don't want to waste it discussing non-sensical stuff. I need to say my piece. I'm sorry I hurt you. And yes, I mean both physically and emotionally. I wanted to make it up to you. Give you the future you deserve. But it doesn't look like I'll get that chance. I—"

"Aiden, don't. It's ancient history." Ann cringed. She didn't want to hear it.

"But do you forgive me?"

"Of course, I do. A part of me will always care about you. But I don't want to mislead you, Aiden. I stopped being *in* love with you the moment you slugged me."

She paused. That wasn't the whole truth. With death looking imminent, she needed to know her slate was completely clear, her heart pure. There was no reason to lash out at Aiden. He had tried to warn then help her. "Truth is, I know now we weren't good together. Looking back, I see I was coming to that conclusion long before you ... *we* had that awful incident. It wasn't you that was wrong for me as much as *we* were wrong for me."

Aiden exhaled a sound of dismay. "I suppose you're right. Neither one of us ever seemed content. Are you with someone else now?"

Ann hesitated as thoughts of Logan flooded her mind. The way he'd hugged Ginny. Teased Don and Barrett. Showed compassion for her mother. Harbored devotion and loyalty for helping the SEALS, despite it being mostly a part of his past. She liked how he threw his passion into his home. She could imagine him working with wood, turning mere boards into floors and walls. Into homes. She had never met anyone like him. In a span of mere days, they had been up close and frank with one another, sharing histories and personal thoughts that in other relationships may have taken weeks to surface.

But was she *with* him? That was the question Aiden had posed. "This isn't about anyone else. It's about me. But in answer to your question, I don't know. I think so. I'm not sure how he feels, but this whole ordeal has made me regret not telling him what was happening in my heart. How special he has become to me." Her eyes watered and a sob slipped through her lips "Now, I'll never get that chance."

A noise filtered in from outside the door. A soft creaking like that of a shoe. *So close!*

Was this it? The end?

Dread penetrated into Ann's bones.

LOGAN ROUNDED the doorframe in a blink, holding a pistol at eye level, both arms extended, pointing directly at them. He was fully prepared to shoot anyone besides Ann in the room.

Before she and the unknown occupant tethered in the other chair could utter a reaction to his appearance, he jerked his upper torso side to side, assessing the room, looking for other people. Empty. Not even a window or a door. He lowered his weapon and hurried to Ann. His stomach knotted at the site of the bruises on her face.

"Logan!" Ann sounded as startled as she was relieved. "But how—"

The stranger exhaled deeply. "Logan, whoever you are, I have never been so happy to see anyone in my life!"

As Logan pulled a knife from his pocket and cut the tape binding Ann, she said, "How did you know to find me here?" As soon as her hands were free, she threw her arms around him in a quick bear hug.

"Umm, help me out here," the stranger added, sounding a little panicked.

"Who's he?" Logan gestured toward the guy as he cut the tape from her feet.

"Aiden. Here," Ann said reaching for the knife. "I'll cut him loose. You can guard the door. We think the guy who's behind all this will be back any second."

Logan lifted his pistol to be at the ready again and strode to the doorframe while Ann scurried to cut the remaining bindings. "Aiden? As in Aiden Rutherford?"

"Yes," Ann said, "and why he's here is a long story. We can discuss that later."

"But you're convinced he was never involved in any of this?" Logan shifted a gaze from the warehouse to toss a doubtful scowl at Aiden.

"Yes, I'm—" Ann began.

Aiden lifted his head in defiance and glared back at Logan. "Hellooooo, I'm right here. I didn't have anything to do with this!" He sounded affronted. "I wouldn't hurt Ann for anything—" He broke off when Logan arched an eyebrow at him. "Oh, I see she told you about that one time. Look, I—"

"Aiden, not now." Ann finished cutting his bindings then stood. "We can deal with that later." She offered the knife back to Logan, but he gestured for her to hold onto it. She nodded in acquiescence. "How did you find me?"

"The recording of you and Sam. That led me to his place then Tracy's apartment. I saw her brother, George Clemens, in a picture with her. It was taken a few years back, here in the Anacostia district."

"Anacostia! That's where we are now?" Ann rubbed her forehead. "Never mind, we can go through all this later. Can we just get out of here?" She sounded panicked.

"That's the plan." Logan kept his gaze on the storage area outside the door. "First, tell me, was he alone all the time? Did you see or hear anyone else? Did he talk about any other person being involved in this?"

"No," Ann was quick to respond. "He never mentioned anyone

else. But he swore he wasn't the one who set the explosion at Lube-Royal. So, there may be others out there somewhere."

Logan nodded slowly, like he was sorting through her words. "I think he's telling the truth about that." His gaze continued to dart around the warehouse as they spoke. "Are there any other exits on this floor besides the double doors on the other side?" He gestured to clarify the direction he meant. "And I don't mean roll-up doors, they would be too noisy."

"I don't know. I was drugged and woke up here." She looked at Aiden.

Aiden shrugged a shoulder. "That's the only exit I know of."

"There have to be more," Logan said, reasoning out loud. "This is a warehouse. Fire codes dictate at least one more. But we don't have time to search, so we'll have to take our chances on that one and head back out the alley."

He hesitated and pulled the second pistol from his back waistband, disengaging the safety. He wanted to place it in Ann's hands, wanted her to have protection. But more than that, he needed to sandwich her between himself and Aiden as a safety barrier. He flicked his gaze to Aiden. He had no choice but to trust this guy. "Can you handle a pistol?"

Aiden hesitated, looking at it like it was a snake. His gaze leaped to Ann before looking at Logan. A voice full of puffed bravado, he said, "Of course, I can." He took the gun.

"Safety's off, so be careful." Logan eyed him a moment longer then looked at Ann, beckoning her to follow. He touched his finger to his lips to remind them to move quietly then leaned toward them to whisper, "Stick together. Ann in the middle."

She nodded. He momentarily gripped her hand to offer assurance. Her lips curled into a weak smile.

He stepped silently out into the storage area, leading with his gun. Moving slowly to keep the group together, he stopped to listen intently every few yards.

They rounded pile after pile of stacked crates, moving steadily toward the stairwell and then the exit that would lead to the alley.

Logan scoured his mind for strategy. How long before the police found them? How soon would Clemens return? What would they do once they were in the alley? If Clemens cornered them there, they would be sitting ducks.

Once at the door that lead into the passageway backing to the stairwell, Logan motioned for the other two to stop and listen.

Silence.

He gestured for them to stand to the side. They acquiesced without saying a word.

As he reached for the door, Aiden whispered, "Wait!"

Logan lurched back, looking frantically in every direction then at him. Nothing seemed untoward. "What! Wait for what?"

Aiden offered a sheepish look then cast his gaze at Ann before returning it to Logan. "I need to use the restroom," he said gesturing over his shoulder at a door near them.

Logan squinted at the man. "Now? You want to use it *now*?" They needed to get to the exterior doors as soon as possible before Clemens returned!

"Hey, I drank a thirty-two-ounce diet soda on my way here," he hissed. "That was hours ago. You try going that long without ... don't make me embarrass my—"

Logan sighed. "All right, go on." As annoyed as he was, it was hard to keep his voice at a whisper. "We'll move on to the exterior doors. Just get there as fast as you can."

Aiden nodded quick jerks and hurried into the restroom.

Logan took a steadying breath then inched open the door to the passageway with his free hand and hastened through, once again ready to shoot if necessary.

The passage was empty. Only a few more yards to the exterior doors. "Come on," he said to Ann. She followed on his heels. They repeated the cautious approach in going through the stairwell door as well.

The exterior doors were just ahead about a yard to his left. They were made of metal except for square windows about two feet by two feet on their upper third.

He stepped to them intending to look through the glass, but a scuffle and a small squeak of terror sounded from behind him. He whirled around, pistol raised, to see Clemens holding Ann tight against his chest, a revolver wedged snug into the underside of her jaw. He must have been hiding a few steps up in the stairwell!

"Lower the gun, hero," Clemens snarled through a crooked smirk.

Logan complied, dropping his arms.

"Atta boy," Clemens chuckled. "Now slowly put the pistol on the ground and slide it to me. Just like they do on cop shows."

For the briefest second, Logan hesitated. Would Clemens hurt Ann if he refused to surrender the gun? Where was Aiden? *Please let him be smart enough to watch ahead and create a distraction.* If he did, Logan could overpower Clemens.

"Now!" Clemens ordered.

Seeing no recourse, Logan did as he was told. He couldn't take chances that the guy might explode and punish Ann for his act of defiance.

Once the pistol reached Clemens's feet, he removed his grip from Ann long enough to bend down, scoop it up, and plunk it into his belt.

"Now you. Get down there," Clemens said gesturing with his gun toward the floor. "On your stomach."

Again, Logan hesitated. *Where was Aiden?* Finally, seeing no recourse, he did as he was told.

"You won't get away with this," Logan said. "The police are on their way. Your whole plan is ruined. If you hurt Ann, they'll know you did it. Tracy's not going to end up with Sam. She won't have any money to share with you. You're not helping her at this point. You're making things worse for—"

"Shut up and let me think!" Clemens dragged Ann backward to look out the doors' small windows. "Where's that other buddy of yours, honey, eh? Did you leave him tied up or is he lurking around here with a gun, too?"

When Ann didn't answer, he shook her.

"I don't know where he is!" she snapped. "Probably on the cell phone with the police right now giving them our exact location." Her voice sounded both shaky and obstinate.

Logan was proud of her. She was no fool. She was cooperating but fighting back in her own way. She sounded one part in control and one part scared to death. Both parts made him want to draw her into his arms. Protect her. He felt a surge of savage anger at Clemens for causing her such distress and danger. "She's right," he added from the floor. "The police only needed to know which building we were in and your license plate number. Now they know both."

"I said shut up!" Clemens roared. "Besides, it's circumstantial evidence. That's all they've got. Your word against mine. But I'm not staying here. You're coming with me."

Logan heard Ann whimper, confirming Clemens had spoken to her.

"You're my only ticket out of this mess," Clemens added.

Logan panicked. Clemens was getting desperate. Abandoning his plans and switching to escape. By taking Ann hostage! But if he tried to overpower Clemens now, the louse might shoot her straight away.

"You hear that?" He kicked Logan in the side. "I'm taking her, so don't think of trying to follow me, or I might get mad and take it out on her." He kicked again, smack-dab in the spot that had been injured at the hospital. "You count to a hundred slowly before you get up, hero. If I hear a sound from this door before I'm gone, I might get mad and make her pay."

Clemens opened the exterior door and pushed Ann through.

After the door closed behind them, Logan scrambled to his feel as he heard something being wedged in the doors' handles. He inched to the window and watched as Clemens shoved Ann toward the van. *Don't get in Ann; don't do it.* He wanted to pound on the door. Break it down. However, given Clemens's deranged orders, he didn't dare. He studied the alley, trying to figure out some way to stop that van.

Behind him the door leading into the passageway opened, and he heard Aiden say, "Okay, I'm ready now ..." Then, "Where's Ann?"

"Clemens got her!"

"Don't just stand there!" Aiden bellowed as he moved. "Let's go after her!"

Before Logan could stop him, Aiden shoved past and moved to the exterior doors.

He pushed on the door but it wouldn't budge. Putting his face snug to the window, he searched the alley for Ann.

ONCE SHE HAD BEEN HUSTLED to the outside, Ann watched as Clemens stepped away a few feet toward a pile of broken pallets. She put her hand to her jawline where he had jammed the gun. The impact of the cold metal on her skin had made her think of death itself.

With his free hand, Clemens picked up a rotted 2x4 piece of wood and shoved it in the handles of the exterior doors.

Ann's gaze veered away, darting every direction, searching for escape. No one else was in sight, but there were shadows everywhere. Dark shadows. Unfortunately, no movement. And as long as he had the gun on her ...

Clemens stomped to her and shoved her forward again, gesturing toward a van. "Get in. You're driving."

As slowly as she dared, she moved toward the van, glancing back at the warehouse doors, wishing, hoping ...

Run? Wouldn't that be better than taking a chance of climbing in the van? She was certain she'd never make it out of that van alive again.

I have no chance if I go with him. She wouldn't be able to reason with him. Nothing she could say or do would make a difference to him now.

He was too scared, too far gone mentally. Too unhinged to understand how he was making things worse for his sister. Still, Ann sought for something, anything, she could say or do to change his mind.

Nothing.

She pretended to stumble, trying to slow things down. This grueling death march to the van was going too fast. *Where are the police?* "I'd rather use you as a hostage so I can get away. But I'll shoot you right here if I have to," Clemens warned, pushing her again. "You don't seem to get it. If you and Webb die, then Sam will get the entire business, and he'll leave his wife. Tracy's smart. She'll make sure it happens. She'll send me money. I'll be living fine in Brazil."

Ann glared at him, and saw that he meant it. Her heart thumped wildly. "Even if you kill me, you can't get away. You can't get on a plane. You'll be on the run the whole way to the Mexican border." Her voice was only a semblance of the original.

"It's simple. Take the backroads and keep changing vehicles. They'll never catch me." His tone held a hint of a chuckle. Despite the night sky darkening quickly, she could see his eyes glint ominously. Her blood ran cold.

A lump was lodging in her throat, but she managed to speak anyway. "Please don't hurt me. I never did anything to you. I have a mother who needs me." If begging for her life would save it, she was willing. Besides, anything that bought her time might be helpful.

He made a contemptuous sound. "Boohoo. You sound pathetic."

Behind them a sound came. Someone rattling the exterior doors to the warehouse! Clemens whirled and stepped toward the sound, firing twice. The sound echoed in the narrow alley.

A thousand prompts in her head screamed at her to run. Despite feeling dizzy and weak, Ann forced herself into motion and sprinted in the opposite direction.

Within seconds, bullets zinged at her.

CHAPTER TWELVE

Logan watched Aiden approach the exterior double doors and push, thrusting them open about two inches until the 2x4 thwarted further effort. "Watch out!" he yelled and leaped, hoping to tackle Aiden to the ground before Clemens saw him. Simultaneously, a gun sounded. A bullet soared through the narrow opening between the two doors.

They fell to the ground, Aiden clutching his arm.

In a crazed voice, Aiden shrieked. "I've been hit!"

Logan rolled to his knees, ripped Aiden's sleeve, and assessed the damage. "It's just a flesh wound. The bullet grazed the skin. Could have been much worse. It'll hurt for a while, but you won't need surgery."

Aiden's face drained of color. "I would have been hit in the chest if you hadn't tackled me. He paused then added, "Thank you," as though it didn't come easy to him.

"Just stay down. Clemens said he'd shoot Ann if we—"

More gun shots sounded.

Panicked, Logan scrambled to his feet and edged to the door's window.

"What are you doing?" Aiden admonished. "You just said—"

"Those shots were directed away from us." Logan's words were rushed as he looked out the window. "It's Ann! She broke loose. She's running."

Logan darted his gaze down the alley, looking for another means of escape. The building running parallel had several doors and appeared to be attached by way of the corridor they were in. If he climbed to a higher floor, might he be able to enter that building and work his way to another exit?

No way to find out but to try. He turned and hustled to the stairs.

"Where ya' going?" Aiden's voice revealed fear. He had scooted his body a couple feet to lean against an interior way.

"To find another exit. You'll be fine. He won't be back. Lay low." Logan turned to go, but Aiden stopped him.

"Wait!" Aiden leaned over as much as the pain in his arm seemed to allow. With his free hand, he retrieved Logan's pistol. "Take this. You might need it."

Logan took the gun with a nod of agreement "Let's hope not." He hurried up the steps, taking them two at a time.

ANN MOVED her legs as fast as she could go. She was panting, and her heart was beating so loudly in her ears she couldn't hear anything else.

Run, run, run! It doesn't matter where. Just go!

Thank goodness she was wearing comfortable clothes her mother had brought her, and not the oversized ones Tia had loaned her or a suit and heels.

Every instinct in her wanted to dash in as straight a line as possible just to get to the corner, round it, and disappear. But she made a better target sticking to a straight path, so she zig-zagged her way down the alley as best she could. Still, the bullets seemed to nip at her heels with every step she took.

But that had to be her imagination, didn't it? *I should have counted the bullets! Wouldn't he have to reload soon?*

Too late to worry about that! Just run!

In moments, she rounded the corner to her right and spotted an open door about twenty yards ahead in the building running parallel to where she'd been held prisoner. The door was held ajar with the aid of an empty liquor bottle. No doubt punks or street gangs had worked their way in at some point. Or maybe homeless people sought it as a refuge against the cold.

Didn't matter! She would take her chances with any of them over Clemens any day.

She braved a quick glance over her shoulder and saw him clear the corner. Her hopes bottomed—he would see her enter this door!

She had no choice. She had to get off the straight path she was on. She swung the door wider and dashed inside.

Once in, she had two options. Climb the steps or take her chances with the door to the right. She chose the door.

It was the wrong choice. It was locked. She loathed turning back around to go to the steps, but she had no choice. She raced up them two at a time. As she cleared the first sweep and stepped onto a landing, she heard the exterior door open and Clemens enter.

"You won't escape me!" He bellowed. "Did you hear? You won't get away. You're just making me angrier."

She hurried up the next sweep of steps and stopped at a door.

Locked!

Was this her fate? To be killed in a stairwell? She cried out in dismay, turned, and headed to the third floor where, she noted with fear, the stairs ended.

Please let this door be open! It had to be. Whoever had broken in and propped the door open had to have gone beyond the stairwell, hadn't they?

She put her hand on the handle and yanked.

Success! Opening it wide, she dashed into complete darkness.

When Logan heard distant noises—a metal door slamming, a steady thudding cadence as if from someone running—he stopped in his tracks. After he had climbed the stairwell, he had entered a room so dark it revealed only varying shades of black. Judging by the echoes of the sounds of his own footsteps and the click when the door shut behind him, he figured he was in one large cavernous storage area.

He had taken out his cell phone and used its flashlight feature to guide his stepping. He was intent on finding another way to return to street level. He just hoped he would be in time to find Ann.

Please let me get there in time to help her.

But sounds came from the other side of the vast area. Could it be Ann? Or was it just street punks doing whatever it was they do best?

He clicked off his phone and pocketed it, not wanting the flashlight to give away his location. He didn't dare take the chance of calling out Ann's name. If she had entered the building, she might be placed in further jeopardy by acknowledging his voice.

He stayed still, listening. Footsteps. Hurried footsteps. Heavy breathing. A thwack followed instantly by a startled sound. The voice sounded high-pitched, female. *Could she have walked into something in the dark? Or had someone seized her?* No, if the latter then he ought to have heard a scream and a scuffle.

He inched in the direction of the shuffling feet. So far, so good. The sound of shoes patting on the ground came from only two feet.

That changed in an instant. A loud thud sounded, like that of a door being wrenched open at full strength by someone in a hurry. *A furious person in a hurry.*

"I know you're in here!" A voice bellowed.

Clemens! Logan's heart raced, knowing Ann was somewhere out there, in the dark, somewhere between him and Clemens. She had no weapon. He had to get to her first!

He inched forward, keeping his right side to the exterior wall, stopping to listen every few steps.

"There has to be a light in here," Clemens growled.

His heavy footsteps dissipated, suggesting he may have stopped to listen.

Logan couldn't hear the lighter sounds of Ann's footsteps anymore.

"I told you," Clemens snarled full volume, "if you cause me more trouble, I'll kill you. That hero of yours is probably dead. And the other one was a weakling anyway."

A scuffling sound came from close by, followed by a faint whimper.

He looked for moving shapes. The darker ones to his left suggested piles of crates positioned in long rows, much as they had been in the other warehouse.

He waited. Silence. Then, he spotted a shape of varied degrees of black drawing near. The faintest smell of citrus reached his nostrils.

Ann!

He moved quickly toward the shape, and in a voice as low as possible, whispered her name.

He heard a quick intake of breath and watched Ann's form appear in front of him so close they would have crashed had he not grabbed her forearm to hold her steady. Her arms went around him and she whispered, "Logan."

Despite their situation, despite the loaded gun in his hand, he returned the hug. He thought he felt the brush of her lips on his neck.

"Stay behind me," he whispered, pulling back, "and hold on." He felt her hand clasp his back waistband.

From behind him, he heard a door open. The door he had come through! He tensed. *Please don't let that be Aiden coming in here!*

Overhead, fluorescent lights flickered on, flooding the entire third floor with light. Once his eyes adjusted, Logan saw Clemens about twenty-five feet away, facing them. Clemens raised his gun and his lips shot into a sinister smile when they made eye contact.

Clemens had caught them while Logan's guard was down.

Logan twisted, grabbed Ann's hand and yanked her to the side, crashing into a stack of crated boxes. The boxes rocked. Logan could tell they were about to fall and he shoved Ann from their path as the heavy load spilled to the floor, knocking him down in the process. Pain shot through his right shoulder, and he lost his grip on the pistol.

"Logan!" Ann's voice rang out, sounding horrified.

So many things happened in the next instant, he couldn't be sure in what order things transpired. He couldn't sit up to look either, his torso captured under the weight of heavy wood boxes.

Multiple footsteps scurried from somewhere. A gunshot sounded, too close for comfort. One—maybe two—people yelled. A scuffle followed. He heard a grunt, several thuds, an exhalation, a curse.

He tried to move but couldn't.

A scream sounded, this one making him think it had practically been ripped from Ann's throat.

Terror raced through him. He yelled her name.

Next, came more scuffling as if from more feet racing into the room.

A silence descended but was broken quickly by gasps of relief and satisfaction. Seconds later, more shapes and shadows loomed out of nowhere. From his position on the ground—his view obstructed by heavy boxes, which were getting heavier by the second—he could see the lower halves of people. *Uniformed men and women!* Half a dozen, at least.

But who was shot? He strained his head high enough to see Ann's legs and sneakers. She was still standing. That was all he needed to know as he felt the load on him being lightened bit by bit.

He laid back and everything went black.

ANN WATCHED LOGAN WAKE UP. They were in the back of an ambulance, parked outside the warehouse, doors open wide. Logan lay on a stretcher fully clothed. The EMTs had said his only wound might be a concussion, but they were taking him to the hospital for observation and an X-ray to ensure no bones or vital organs had been damaged.

He blinked several times. The light was dim, but it was probably too bright for his eyes because he opened them only a slit.

"Hey," he said, offering a crooked smile and reaching for her hand. "You okay?"

Through misted eyes, she grinned and took his hand in both of hers. "I am now that you've woken. You gave me an awful fright."

He emitted a soft chuckle, and it drifted, slow and rich, making her throat catch. "That makes two of us. When Clemens had that pistol at your jaw ..." His broke off, not finishing his thought.

She nodded, kissed his hand, and placed it at his side. "Let's not think about it now." *In fact, if we never talk about it again that will be fine.*

He looked toward the open back door of the ambulance as though assessing his surroundings. Ann tracked his gaze to see blinking red lights, police, and EMTs filling the view.

"Clemens?" Logan asked, his brow arched.

Ann cringed. "Shot in the chest. He's already been rushed to the hospital."

Commotion at the door drew their gazes again. They watched as Aiden climbed in with them, folding onto the stretcher opposite and letting loose a deep exhale. A white gauze bandage covered the wound on his upper arm. His face was paler than usual and his eyes revealed fatigue.

"You're awake," Aiden said, meeting Logan's gaze.

It wasn't a question. It was a comment stating the obvious, but Logan nodded anyway. "I guess I owe you a thank you."

Aiden's head jerked back, his gaze darting from Logan to Ann and back. "For what?" His faced flushed. "Given everything that happened here today, I think I caused more harm than good."

"For having a clear head, quick responses, and enough nerve to pick up my gun when I lost hold on it. Mostly, for shooting Clemens."

Aiden gave Ann a sheepish look. "It wasn't me who shot Clemens." Aiden slouched back against the side of the ambulance. Ann watched as a long shudder shook him. "I wasn't quick or focused enough do to it."

Logan studied him. "Then, who?"

Ann cleared her throat. "I shot him."

"You?" Logan studied her, his blue eyes searching her face. "You shot Clemens?" He frowned. "I'm sorry it had to come to that."

Ann shrugged. "I would have preferred not to, but given the circumstances, I'd do it again. I wasn't ready to die, and I was so afraid he would hurt you. He had to be stopped." Her voice broke on a sob and she leaned toward him. He levered to a sitting position and wrapped an arm around her as best as he could, given their awkward positions.

"Ahem," Aiden said. "Awkward moment here."

Ann pulled from Logan's arms and turned to him. "I'm sorry, Aiden, but I told you I don't have feelings for you anymore."

He frowned. "I understand." His voice resonated both disappointment and acceptance.

An EMT climbed into the back. "We're getting ready to go, Miss."

"Oh, of course." Ann got to her feet. "I'll get to the hospital as soon as I can."

Logan looked at the EMT. "Why can't she ride with us?"

Ann extended a stopping hand toward Logan. "No, it's my choice, Logan. I already told him I wouldn't be going along."

"Why? Where are you going?"

"To the police station. An Officer Semansky told me Detective Redding ... remember him from Baltimore? ... Redding wanted us to know he summoned both Sam and Jonathan Tate to the local precinct. I want to be there for that discussion. I'm riding with Officer Semansky."

"Bromberg and Tate? Both at the station? I'm riding with you," Logan said climbing slowly too his feet.

"But you need to go to the hospital!" Ann glared, anxiety for him coursing through her chest.

Logan looked at the EMT. "Am I in imminent danger? Couldn't I go to the police station first and then make an appearance at the hospital afterward?"

The young EMT sighed. "No one can make you go with us now if you don't want to. Just make sure you get an X-ray as soon as possible." He shifted his gaze to Ann. "Keep your eye on him. My concern is possible concussion."

"Will do." Ann turned to Aiden. "Thank you. I know you meant to be helpful." She leaned over and kissed him on the cheek. "Take good care in your new life."

Ann helped Logan climb out of the ambulance. The doors closed after their departure, and Ann never looked back.

LOGAN LEANED AWAY from a hysterical Tate and rubbed his temples. The man was despicable, the way he rationalized his greedy behavior. If they weren't in the police station right now, he might be tempted to punch the guy.

Around him, everyone postured anger—faces flushed, arms flailed, fingers pointed, and voices competed to be heard.

Ann rhythmically jabbed her finger into Sam's chest while she lectured him about what a louse he was. Tracy stood with them, yelling at Sam for leading her on and making her think they had a future. Sam, in turn, was dumping his fury at Tracy, calling her an idiot for thinking he'd ever leave his wife for her. Simultaneously he tried to deliver sweet talk to Ann to get back into her good graces. Tate was furious that his name was being linked to Ann's abduction and barked at Logan for not doing as he had been told.

Finally, a whistle sounded. A human whistle. One of those fingers-in-the-mouth wails that never fails to gain attention.

All voices stopped. Gazes shifted to the whistler, Detective Redding.

"Now that I have your attention," he drawled, "we're going to proceed peacefully into the conference room to your left. No talking. Just go in and take a seat."

Tracy stomped her foot. "Why do I have to go? I had nothing to do with any of this."

"Ms. Harrell," Redding growled. He pointed to the conference room rather than say more. She huffed, but acquiesced.

Redding brought up the rear, shutting the door behind them. "Now, let's—"

"Are we being held for something?" Tate demanded. "If so, then I'm not saying a word until I call my attorney."

Redding sighed. "Nobody is being held for anything yet, Mr. Tate. This is a fact-finding discussion. However, if you are concerned about your involvement, then it is your prerogative to have legal representation present. If so, you'll be removed from the room until such time your attorney arrives."

Tate turned red, his face pulled tight. "What! Then I won't know what's being said here."

"That's the chance you'll take," Redding said, his tone indulgent.

Tate slapped a hand on the table. "Fine," he snapped. "Proceed ... just hurry it along. Some of us have important things to do."

Redding squinted at the man before looking back at the others.

"Let's start with the explosion at LubeRoyal since that seems to be when things first went awry."

Tracy said, "I can save you time, detective. I had nothing to do with that explosion. It was Sam Bromberg and Jonathan Tate. My brother is innocent as well."

Sam jerked around to stare at her. "Shut up! You don't know what you're talking about."

Tracy turned her gaze from Sam and spoke to the detective. "It's not the first time either. He was involved in causing an explosion at another company, too. Standard Chemical, I believe. He said it would profit CRS tenfold. That's what he said," she added as though it bore repeating." She shot Sam a 'gotcha' look.

Detective Redding looked at Sam. "Is that true Mr. Bromberg? Mind you, things will go easier for you if you come clean on your own."

Sam jerked his head in several directions like his neck hurt. His gaze shifted to the ceiling before he spoke. "Yes, fine. I was aware that these incidents were going to occur. I ... ah, well I may have planted the idea with the VP at Standard Chemical and with Tate at Lube-Royal, but I'm not the one who carried them out!"

"This is preposterous," Tate bellowed. "I'll sue you for slander," he said pointing at Sam.

Logan reeled his gaze to Tate. "How could you do that? You have murder on your hands. All for what? To become president and CEO? Is that what you wanted?"

Tate pounded the table. "I didn't kill anyone! I may have arranged for a little damage to the property, but I certainly never authorized anyone getting hurt. It was supposed to be simple. An incident would occur, and CRS would come in and help us clean up the mess. Meanwhile, the company's insurance would take care of everything."

Logan issued a sound of disdain. "And you'd look like the hero for having brought in CRS and saving the day? The problem is, Ann was a little too good. She was going to restore LubeRoyal's reputation before the incident hit international headlines. But you wanted as much exposure as you could get, didn't you?"

Tate looked flummoxed. "What's the matter with that? There's nothing wrong with being ambitious. Too bad our blood ties didn't put a little competitive spirit and ambition in you!" He pointed his finger handgun at Logan and pretended to fire it—his nonverbal for, *I win, with the last word on the subject.*

Logan shook his head. The man was impossible. "Yes, you're right. We couldn't be more different. The problem, Uncle Jonathan ..." he said Tate's name in as condescending a tone as he could manage, "is that your ambition has made you an accessory to murder."

Tate turned beat red with anger. "What!" His gaze jerked to the detective.

"He's right," Detective Redding confirmed.

Tate paused. Blinked. "Fine, but I'm not taking all the blame. It was Bromberg's idea in the first place. He put me in touch with the same man he hired to do the Standard Chemical job."

Sam barked, "Shut up," at Tate. "You sure were quick to run with the idea. Had to prove you were a big man who could save the day. Thought they'd make you CEO of the whole shebang."

Tate's face turned beet red. "Now, see here. I've long earned that title. It should have been mine—"

Detective Redding looked up from where he had been writing and yelled, "Enough."

The room quieted again.

Redding's gaze shifted between Tate and Bromberg. "I'll need the name and contact number of the thug ... or thugs ... you hired."

Both hesitated then nodded. Sam grumbled, "I have it in my office. I want it on record that I'm offering to cooperate."

Redding looked at his notes. "At this point it looks like you both are facing some serious charges. But now I want to know what the explosion has to do with the attacks and subsequent kidnapping of Ms. McCarthy."

Sam piped up first. "I know nothing about it. That's Tracy's doing."

Tracy jerked to upright as though the back of her chair had suddenly sprouted thorns. "I didn't do anything! I simply told my brother what Sam was going to do, and he decided to take advantage of the opportunity." Tears surfaced in her eyes. "He's a little misguided maybe, but he loves me. He was only trying to make sure I was okay. If Sam came into money, then he could leave his wife—" Her gaze darted to Sam and her voice grew harsh "—which he promised to do many times ... to be with me."

Sam snarled, "I never promised any such thing."

Tracy started to counter him but the detective called quiet again. "So, Ms. Harrell, you knew an explosion was about to occur but you told no authorities. You also knew that your brother had taken steps ... kidnapping, attempted murder, shooting Webb Hollis ... but you notified no one. We call that an accessory, also."

Tracy whimpered and slouched back in her chair.

The detective shifted his gaze to Logan. "Mr. Kassell." Then, to Ann. "Ms. McCarthy. You two are free to go with our thanks for being patient and cooperating in this investigation. The rest of you will remain here." He continued over the sound of several huffs and curses. "You are being booked for some rather serious offenses. All this must be coordinated with the District police so this will take some time." He turned and shoved a stopping hand at Tate. "And yes, Mr. Tate, you'll be given a chance to call your attorney."

Tate merely scowled back in return.

Ann helped Logan stand. He shook the detective's hand.

"Remain available," Redding told them. "There are still many details we have to unearth."

They nodded. Logan said, "You know how to reach us."

Within minutes they were on the sidewalk outside the police station, heading to Logan's Bronco.

After progressing several yards, Logan said, "It's funny ... Clemens and Tate couldn't be more different in their social and professional circles, yet their personalities are almost identical. Greedy, selfish, driven by blind ambition. It's almost uncanny."

ANN STOPPED IN HER TRACKS, placed a hand on his arm, and stepped close so they were eye to eye. Oblivious to the world around her, she studied his face while streams of people eddied past. "You know what else is uncanny? That I haven't thanked you yet."

He placed his hand on hers where it rested on his arm. "For what?"

157

"For saving my life. For making me feel special. For the glimpse into your wonderful life and—"

He interrupted her by leaning forward and kissing her on the lips. "Funny, I was wondering how in the world I would ever thank you. I'm sorry your affiliation with LubeRoyal not only threatened your life but probably cost you the opportunity to cash out of CRS in eighteen months."

She sighed. "Oh that." She brushed it away with her hand. "It seems so minor compared to your situation. Do you think Tate will ever grant you custody now that his dreams have been destroyed?"

Logan tensed. "I don't know. I guess we'll have to wait and see. All I can do now is deal with the present. So, in that vein ... first thing tomorrow ..." He checked the time on his cell phone. "... or later this morning, we need to get you a new cell phone."

Ann chuckled. "I appreciate it, but that can wait. I believe we're due at the emergency room."

Logan shook his head. "The cell phone can't wait. I intend to see a whole lot more of you, and you'll need a phone to receive my calls." He pulled her into his arms. "Would that be all right with you?"

Before she could respond, he added, "I heard what you told Aiden before I stepped into the room at the warehouse. That you regret not telling this other man in your life what was happening in your heart and how special he had become. I hope I am that other man. If so, then you need a phone so that you can tell me again and again and again. Do you think that's possible?" He offered a grin and looked at her expectantly. *Please let her say yes.*

Ann's skin pinked and her lips twisted in a mischievous way. "No, it's more than possible ... I'd say it's highly probable."

He jerked his head back as a roar of laughter slipped from his lips. Then, despite his injuries, he pulled her close and lifted her such that her feet dangled above the sidewalk then twirled her around, prompting people on the street to snicker and swing a wide berth to pass around them.

He didn't care what they thought. He was in love with this woman and was elated she made *them* a probability.

EPILOGUE

E*ight months later*
  "Good job!" "Whoot, whoot!"
  "Congratulations!"

A scattering of clapping joined the many voices chorusing compliments around Logan's dining table as Ann finished signing an agreement authorizing Webb to her shares of CRS. After Sam was tried and sentenced, Sam's wife had approached Webb and offered to sell her husband's portion at a price Webb couldn't refuse.

Ann would not pocket as much as she could have had she remained with CRS for the remaining ten months, but the terms were lucrative enough to enable her to pay off the family farm and pad her savings account. Finally, she could afford to launch her new career an independent research journalist.

"Okay, I got you and Webb," her former roommate Miranda said, lowering her camera. She moved closer and crouched down to photograph from a different angle. "Now, one of you alone. Look up at everyone. That's good."

Ann moved her gaze to the crowd of people she loved, scattered around the kitchen-dining area. Logan had insisted they hold the gathering so their friends could participate in her new venture. She had been skeptical about inviting everyone to the top of a Maryland mountain in snowy January, but almost every guest had voiced delight at the view of the winter wonderland spread out below them in the valley.

Her gaze drifted to Logan. He winked and nodded in a way that said, "I'm proud of you."

After taking several more shots, Miranda stood, gave Ann a thumbs-up sign, and turned to talk to their other roommate, Rhea.

In seconds, Webb was at Ann's side again, extending his hand. "We need to make it official."

Ann chuckled and shook his hand. "You sure this is what you want? You talked so often about selling out your interest, too. I hope you're not doing this on my account." He was such a generous man, it would be like him to do that.

"I'm not," Webb assured her. "Now that Sam is out of the picture, joy has returned. I can turn CRS into the company I envisioned in the first place. I just wish I could convince you to stay."

Ann sighed. "I appreciate it. I'll always be around to answer questions or help you brainstorm, but I'm done with CRS. And the travel. And with D.C., for that matter. I love my quieter, more relaxed way of life."

"Your gain is our loss," Rhea said, moving in for a quick hug then shooting an exaggerated pout at Miranda. "Who will cook for us now? We'll starve."

Ann chuckled. Her roommates were far from helpless. She, Miranda, and Rhea were known among their friends in D.C. for being brainy, beautiful, and bold, respectively. Or depending which friend one talked to, focused, fashionable, and feisty. Ann was certain Rhea's boldness and feistiness would see her through any concerns. As for Miranda, she certainly wouldn't starve. She was never at a loss for a dinner date. Both roommates were attractive, but Miranda's long blond hair and regal features never failed to turn heads. Besides, Miranda was the most sociable of the three of them.

"I'm sure you two can figure out how to cook meat. If not, there's always bread and raw vegetables."

Rhea huffed. "We're at the top of the food chain; why would we want to limit our lives to being vegetarians?" she quipped.

Miranda rolled her eyes. "Seriously, Ann, the apartment will never be the same without you. I can't believe you're giving up our fun and craziness for 'quiet and relaxed'."

Webb's wife Tia spoke from across the table. "Relaxed? Hardly. She's on the road most of the time between West Virginia and Smithsburg."

Barrett—despite being mid-chew on a large bite of cake—chimed in, "I can attest to that. Logan's hard to find these days, too."

"That's true," Don added, moving his gaze from his wife Meira and son Ethan to Logan, "we don't see much of him anymore." He paused and shot a lopsided grin at Barrett, "But I noticed you're here a lot more, too ... and at suppertime, as I recall."

"Ahh, the truth comes out." Rhea chuckled. "Perhaps all the research Ann talked about is being done here. With Logan."

Ann felt her face warm as chuckles rang out around the room. It was true. Logan was no longer with LubeRoyal and she had moved back to West Virginia to be with her mom. However, she and Logan burned a significant amount of gas getting together every weekend and sometimes mid-week. Always, Logan would bring Ginny along to visit Delores, and Ann would journey with her mother to satisfy an anxious Ginny. Despite the foursome arrangement, which they all seemed to love, she and Logan managed to sneak in a private date or two each week—picnics, museums, movies, snowmobiling or horseback riding at a nearby stable. Plus, Ginny and Delores kept so busy playing cards, knitting, or cooking, that Ann and Logan found ample time alone together.

"I'm envious," Rhea whispered to Miranda, her voice so low Ann could barely catch what she said. "Do you think we'll ever find a guy as good as Logan? We're not getting any younger, you know." Ann watched Rhea frown. "Maybe we should skip the man and go straight for adoption."

Miranda shot her a look. "Speak for yourself," she whispered. "I'm perfectly content being single. And childless. Besides, my career in fashion photography is really starting to take off. You adopt the kids, and I'll be the auntie who spoils them."

Ann smiled. She would miss her roommates and their banter. But now that she'd fallen in love with Logan, and even with Ginny, she could never go back to her old life. Her mother's voice interrupted her thoughts and she looked up to see Delores McCarthy talking to Tia.

"We are on the road a lot, you're right." She smiled and her eyes twinkled. "But coming here puts such a smile on both my girls' faces. I feel like it's added years to my life. I'm just glad they want me around."

Ann startled. "Mama, of course we do. And with the doctor's latest good report on your health, I feel doubly blessed."

"Yeah, Nana Delores," Ginny said from behind Delores's chair. She leaned forward and hugged her from behind. "I wish you were here all the time."

Logan cleared his throat in one of those unnatural ways that suggested he was determined to get attention. The voices grew quiet. Ann watched his gaze turn to Delores for a moment. She nodded at him with a knowing grin.

"What's going on?" Ann asked.

Logan smiled. "This seems to be the week for good news. As you know ... and despite my uncle's shenanigans ... I finally got custody of Ginny—" He paused as applause broke out. He pulsed his palms at them to let them know there was more. "And Ann has officially started the work she desires. What's more, I had an eye-opening conversation with Delores earlier and it turns out she's not so keen about her West Virginia farm as she is the views of her Appalachian Mountains."

Ann cocked her head. *What in the world was he talking about?*

"Which," Logan continued, "happen to be some of the same mountains we see in the distance from the veranda here." He looked pointedly at Ann.

Ann darted her gaze to her mother.

Delores nodded at her, "It's true, dear."

Baffled, Ann shifted her gaze back to Logan. He and her mother had talked about this. Why? What were they plotting?

"So," Logan said, "it's time to make this happiness go full circle. He stepped close to Ann. "I'm tired of driving. So are you. And so is Delores. She's agreed that living here would suit her just fine. She plans to rent out the family farm."

Ann shook her head. "What are you talking about?"

"Oh!" A squeal rang out. Ann recognized it as Miranda's voice. Then, her friend mumbled something about seeing a photographic moment coming, and where was her camera?

But Ann ignored Miranda. Her gaze remained glued, in confusion, on Logan.

Before she could take another breath, he dropped to one knee while turning over his hand to reveal a small ring box. "Anna Grace McCarthy, I don't want to spend another day without you by my side." He opened the box. "You've made me a better man and I need you in my life. Will you marry me?"

As Miranda snapped pictures, moisture flooded Ann's eyes, and she put a hand over her mouth to stifle a cry. Before she could answer, Ginny squealed. "Oh, Anna Grace! Say yes. Please say yes!"

Logan shot Ginny a quelling look before shifting his gaze back to Ann.

Overwhelmed, Ann took a deep breath to make sure she could talk coherently. "Of course, I will," she said, cupping the sides of his face in her hands and pulling him into a kiss.

Cheers broke out around the table as he inched the ring onto her third finger.

Logan stood, pulling Ann to her feet and sealing the deal with a kiss. But, it was brief, because he quickly leaned back and added, "Wait a second. I have one condition."

She arched a brow. "What might that be?"

"Since you decided to turn in that power suit ..." He grinned sheepishly. "I wondered if you'd turn in your power name as well. I'd like our wedding license to say Anna Grace, not Ann. Do you think we can make that happen?"

"Now *that*, is a definite probability." She smiled, stepping back into his arms and knowing full well, she would be his Anna Grace for the rest of her life.

The End

LETHAL CAPERS PREVIEW

Please enjoy this excerpt from
Book 2 in the
Risky Changes Series,
brought to you by: **Brimstone Fiction, LLC**.
Lethal Capers
By
DL Koontz

CHAPTER ONE | LETHAL CAPERS

The last thing Rhea Bohannon wanted to do was stand at a graveside in miserable, muggy weather, pretending to mourn for the louse in the coffin.

It was early morning but already the temperature sweltered. She twisted her neck to shift the sweat-laden collar of her dress from her skin. Late June in humid southeast Georgia was indeed oppressive.

And buggy. She had hoped to attend and put the past behind her, but the stinging sensation on her legs confirmed she would live with the after-effects of the service for several more days, whether she wanted to or not.

She sighed. Why *had* she returned?

To make certain the guy was dead. Truly dead.

She snorted at the thought, and the briefest twinge of guilt washed over her—*the smallest twinge of all twinges, thank you very much*. She lifted her gaze back to the front, summoning more reverence for this final passage. *Whether the un-dearly departed deserved it or not.*

Besides, there was nowhere else of interest to look anyway. She was the lone mourner...nay, scratch that. Make that *attendee;* definitely, not *mourner.* She wasn't surprised no one else attended the service.

Then again, she had hoped to see signs of a new family. Someone.

Anyone. One or two people to help explain what the clod had been doing for the past sixteen years.

More importantly, clues as to *why* he left. After all, he had wanted to leave so badly and so thoroughly that he took on a new name. Frank Murphy. *How unoriginal.*

Rhea watched as the reverend closed his Bible—*finally!*—thereby signaling that the "few words at the gravesite" he'd promised at the onset, were coming to an end. Clearly the pastor had spent time writing a good eulogy for a man he'd never known, and doggone it, he was going to deliver no matter how many people were—or weren't—there.

"Aeschylus wrote," he said, "that there's nothing certain in man's life except this: That he must lose it. We must all seek to make use of our brief journey here as best we can. And as God would lead us."

With that, the Reverend Markel bent his substantial body to the ground and scooped a handful of dry dirt. "Earth to earth, ashes to ashes ..." He continued delivering the full mantra from the Book of Common Prayer, dramatically tossing bits of earth onto the casket with each phrase.

Nice touch. If Rhea had an ounce of grief in her for the jerk in the casket, that ceremonial gesture might have tugged at her heart.

She pulled her shoulders back, gauging herself emotionally. *Nothing.* She felt composed. Good to go.

As the funeral crew continued lowering the coffin into the ground, Rhea's thoughts switched to assessing the actual box that held the remains of her errant father, a man she had not seen or spoken to since she was fourteen years old. Granted, the casket wasn't the inlaid cherry kind with corners of brass she had seen at ritzier funerals, but :t *was* more than a cheap pine box.

Someone had to have paid for it.

But who?

Well, it had not been her. In fact, if an attorney by the name of Richard Avery hadn't phoned and told her about her father's death and his new identity, she wouldn't even have known he was dead.

Kiefer Bohannon. Aka, Frank Murphy. Her father.

Father? Sperm donor and surname-bestower seemed more applicable. *Father* implied caring. Protecting. Being present. He'd struck out on all three.

Rhea took a final deep breath and turned to go, heading south to her car. She'd learned earlier the reverend would ride with the funeral crew on a northbound path, a crude road she hadn't known about beforehand.

She was due at Mr. Avery's office in a few hours. Until then, she had a couple stops to check off her list. It had been twelve years since she'd been in Weld, and she was determined to soak in more of her home town. From the little she had seen earlier that morning, it still appeared large enough to have its own water tower but small enough for rumors to spread from end to end in the time it took to drive the same distance.

She trudged through the rows of towering slash pines, back to where she left her car. The gravesite, like many in the backwoods of this part of southeast Georgia, was old, unadorned, and not easily accessible by vehicle, its surroundings long since taken over by the local pulp mill which would convert the wood into a thick fiber board to be shipped to a paper mill for further processing. The mill was the largest and best-paying employer in the mostly rural county, so people rarely objected to its land encroachments or expansions.

The tall pine woods were patterned into neatly planted rows, but the earthen floor beneath was thick, dark, and shadowed from the canopy of foliage blocking the sun. Still, the hot, humid climate provided the perfect combination for thick, spiky palmetto plants and a multitude of tropical-like vines and other vegetation to flourish.

Rhea stepped with care. She had learned to, long ago. If the jiggers of bramble bushes didn't snag, then there was always a spider or a snake of some sort to guard against.

After about a hundred yards of arduous trekking from the gravesite, the crack of gunfire cut through the air, thundering in her ears. At the same time, she felt something burn her upper arm.

Blasted bugs! She wasn't sure which was worse: being eaten alive by bugs or losing her hearing to hunters. She'd forgotten the mill allowed hunters to use the property.

Then again, it was June. Out of season for hunting deer.

They must be shooting at wild hogs!

She would tackle a bullet or a spider any day over a wild hog. Her heart pulsed a rapid rhythm in her neck as she quickened her step.

An odd rushing whoosh from a moving figure sounded from her left an instant before she was thrust backward with enough force to lift her off her feet. As she fell, her assailant's hands tethered in a vice grip to her torso, she heard another ping of a bullet.

With a mouthful of dirt and several aches she was certain would take days to shake, she tensed as the guy—deduced by the body builder size and the massive amount of muscles gripping her—dragged and rolled her behind a cover of thick vegetation.

Don't panic! Her mind raced, seeking reason. The idiot had merely employed an extreme way of shielding her against wild hogs, that's all. Besides, she was known for being bold and brave. Her two roommates said so often. They were considered brainy and beautiful. But she, LaRhea Bohannon, was bold and brave.

Still, what was he doing here? Why now? And why choose such drastic measures?

What's more, she had not seen or heard a hog...

Anxiety spread through her like dye in water.

Think! Remember those self-defense classes. As a journalist she had conducted many an interview in the seedier parts of Baltimore and Washington D.C. Plus, years of lurking in courtrooms and jails and back allies—where she got her best leads for stories—had prepared her for moments like this. Wild hog or wild criminal, it didn't matter, although she felt safer with the latter.

She knew what she was supposed to do, but the guy held her torso so snug she couldn't free her arms. And his legs were weighing hers down. In the span of a heartbeat or two, he had thrown her to the ground, rolled her several yards, and spread himself on top of her.

With a bravado she didn't feel, she growled, "Get ... off ... of me!"

Before she could blink the man thrust a rough hand over her mouth. "Quiet," he hissed.

She squirmed and tried to knee him in the groin, that vital area she'd been taught would undo a man. No luck, but she did succeed in loosening his grip enough to bite his hand.

"Hey!" he growled, his tone still hushed. "You want to get shot?"

As he spoke she maneuvered loose from his grip and turned her head to stare at him.

Nick Sheehan!

She swallowed back the shock. Here, in the swampy, backwoods regions of Georgia—with bullets zinging by, and her having only been in the area a few hours—she was looking into the face of the guy she once promised to marry!

Nerves thrashing, she demanded, "How did you—"

Gunfire sounded again in rapid succession and wood splinters rained down on them, attesting as to how close the bullets hit.

"What kind of idiot shoots—" she began, but Nick tightened his hold, forcing her to roll with him farther from the spot until they were sheltered by thicker brush. Before she could say more, he yanked her to her feet and commanded in a rushed voice, "Come on!"

One more gunshot sounded as they raced, him holding her hand in a grip that gave her little option but to do as he instructed. Besides his rough control as he dragged her through the woods, she was painfully aware that her arms, face, and one foot—due to losing a shoe along the way—were now scratched by thorns and razor-sharp palm fronds.

All the while, she tried yelling for him to let go, but mostly her words came out as nonsense due to being so winded.

After another couple hundred yards, she finally yanked free of him, and bent over to gulp in air. She didn't like the way he gave orders and liked even less that she'd been forced to follow them.

"Are ... you ... crazy?" she snapped between shuddering gasps of breath. "There's no need to get all Rambo on me."

His head jerked back. "Me, crazy? You didn't notice someone shooting at you?" His voice revealed sarcasm, annoyance. He scowled, shifting his gaze to study the woods behind her shoulder.

She opened her mouth to issue a retort but thought better of it. This was Nick. Once, *her* Nick, the love of her life. He wasn't a danger. He wouldn't play games with her. Sure, their breakup hadn't been any relationship manual's description of how to do it right, but they had never shared harsh words. In fact, they had never shared any words about their ending, given how she headed out of town without saying goodbye.

She swallowed against the cringe-worthy memory of her actions and muttered between breaths, "Nick, it's ... amazing ... to see you ... really, it is. But that was just a ... a lazy hunter who wasn't following safe hunting practices ... and—"

"That was no hunter." Irritation warred in his eyes, and it made her shiver. "Instead of arguing, you should thank me for saving your life back there." He placed a hand at his neck and rolled his head as though easing the kinks he collected from their ordeal in the woods. "Never mind. It's obvious he was only trying to scare you anyway. You're safe. For now."

That neck-head thing he did. That movement. It was so him. In the briefest of moments her mind rushed back fourteen years to pull on a precious memory. Their second date. They were both sixteen and drove to Jekyll Island to swim. He had been determined to impress her with his boogie boarding skills. Unfortunately, he suffered several wipe-outs instead. When he finally dragged himself to shore, he rolled his head and coddled his neck in the same manner. In the two years they continued to date, she learned this mannerism was as natural to him as laughing.

The bittersweet nostalgia of the memory softened her temper. But not her conviction. In a gentler voice, she asked, "For now? What's that supposed to mean?"

Nick paused, then shook his head like he didn't have the right words. When he finally spoke, his voice was flat and emotionless. "Things are going on, that's all."

She raised her eyebrows. "Things? What things? And how in the world did you know I'd be here?"

He hesitated, his jaw tightening and releasing as she waited for an answer. In that respite, she studied him. He was still attractive. *Very* attractive. She'd forgotten how tall he was, six-three to her five-eleven. Same rugged, square jaw. Same hazel eyes and brown hair. Same dimple on both sides of his mouth. But age had blessed him even more. Standing before her now was not the baby face of the eighteen-year-old Nick she'd left behind; this was a chiseled thirty-year-old man with muscles in places he never had before. She noted too that, like her, faint lines now fanned from his eyes and his lips, suggesting exposure to sun and laughter.

At least, she hoped he had experienced laughter, lots of it, given how she had probably hurt him.

He broke the silence. "Look, while you're here, you need to be extremely careful." His tone was indulgent as though talking to a child and he kept returning his attention to the woods behind them. "Sorry about your dad," he added in a gentler tone.

Wow, news does travel quickly in Weld. A shocked laugh escaped her lips. "My dad? Are you kidding? You know what a crud he was to me."

When he didn't respond, she looked up to see his attention still focused on the woods.

"It was just a hunter. If anything, thank you for saving me from a wild hog." As she spoke, her gaze drifted over him again, for the first time noticing a pistol tucked into a holster at his hip. "Wait a minute. You have a gun! Why didn't you save us this crazy race through the woods and use it if we had actually been in danger? Which we weren't."

Nick rubbed two fingers tiredly between his brows. "It's not that simple."

"Why not?" That quickly, a new thought struck. "Oh, I get it. This was payback, wasn't it?" Ice had crawled into her tone.

The rigid lines in his face softened, changing his steely expression. His lips curved upward at the corners and he looked mildly amused. He crossed his arms, his gaze drilling into her. "Payback? For what?"

"For the way I left. For our breakup. For not explaining. You're angry, I get it. You found out I was here and wanted to drag me through ... through ..." She waived an arm wildly, gesturing at the woods behind them. "... Through the mud and the muck and the bugs and the brambles just to get even."

He smirked. "First off, there was no mud." "There could have been!"

"Or muck."

"Nick—"

"Secondly," he said, that grin still lurking, "you haven't changed a bit, have you? Still the same defensive, hot-headed woman you always were. Except you've grown more judgmental and sarcastic through the years. Why would I waste my time with a payback when I'm better off for what happened anyway?"

"Ohhh," she screeched, stomping a foot. Not only was he cheeky and rude, he appeared to be amused by her. "At least I'm not stuck in the middle of nowhere like you. I've moved beyond this rustic wasteland—"

"Rustic wasteland? You used to call it peaceful. Cozy. Has the journalist moved onto a larger vocabulary?"

Seething inside, Rhea spat back, "How did you know I'm a...Yes, I'm a journalist and a darn good one. What are you?" She eyed the pistol again. "The deputy of a two-bit town in a county with enough people to form a baseball team if they're lucky?"

Something ticked in his jaw and he firmed his lips. "As a matter of fact, I am a deputy. Part time. And I'm using it to fight the good fight."

Fight the good fight. From the Bible. The Book of Timothy. A sense of déjà vu flooded through her. He had voiced those words before. Back when they were seventeen. They had planned to attend college together at University of Georgia. Then, he hoped to join the military as an officer and serve his country for four or five years while she traveled with him, as his wife, and worked as an independent reporter for several national news outlets. After that, they wanted to settle down in their hometown of Weld and raise a family. He had been vague about his plans after that, but she had determined to take over the local paper or start her own publication. They'd had such grand plans.

Wistfulness and the innocence of those long-ago dreams filled her core, and she tried to affect a cordial tone. "Look, Nick, I don't want to argue. You look great. Like you're doing well. I'm happy for you. Real happy." The notion of how many times she'd thought about him through the years surged over her. Her stomach clenched with a longing she hadn't felt in a long time, a fleeting glimpse of the happiness they had once shared. She felt like her body might crumble. "In fact, you'll never know how often ..." Her voice cracked.

She caught herself. "Never mind. I'm happy for you. You deserve the best and if being a deputy makes you happy, then that's great. There's probably more to say, but I have a feeling it would just lead to more arguing, so I'm saying goodbye instead. I need to get back to my car. Get some things done."

Besides, I can't handle the way you're looking at me right now, like I'm an alien you don't recognize.

He said nothing, but his eyes flashed like he was holding in a barrage of comments. The result was a stunned pause, cold and tense, as if any residual caring that might have somehow remained from twelve years ago was now gone.

Finally, his gaze dropped to her bare foot. In a resigned voice he said, "My car's up ahead. Wait here and I'll get—"

She put up a stopping hand. "No need. I recognize this spot. My car's right around the bend."

He raked both hands through his hair and fixed her with a tired look. "Then by all means, leave again." His gaze scathed her and his words floated on the hot, stale air like a hiss.

She exhaled a weary breath, hating the heated exchange they had shared. They were two yards and a decade of animosity apart.

So be it. She turned and hobbled away from him, feeling his gaze on her back. Tiny stones spiked into her bare foot every other step.

Why had she come here? Her wayward father wouldn't have cared one smidgeon whether or not she came to his funeral. Sure, she was in a tenuous situation, facing huge decisions back in Maryland. Critical decisions that would impact her future forever after. But she could have addressed that situation from anywhere else.

It was stupid to assume she wouldn't run into Nick as long as she stayed away from the old hangouts. She should have known he would remain in the area. He loved it there. She had, too, but that was long ago.

Once she did see him, it had been silly to expect civility. *I should have known better.* Their footprints were everywhere around this county. Their shadows probably still lurked in the corners of their

hometown of Weld. Their reflections still wavered in the black swamps where they'd gone exploring.

She stumbled on, questioning the wisdom of her plans. She had taken a leave of absence from the *Baltimore Tribune* where she worked as an investigative reporter. Beyond the brief burial, visiting the gravesites of her mom and sister Lily, and meeting with Mr. Avery, her plans included finding bits of the young girl she'd left behind. The happy girl she was before her father abandoned her mother and her when she was fourteen. The idealistic girl that dreamed of settling down with Nick and being owner and editor of their hometown paper. The romantic girl that hoped to watch her own children grow up in a stable environment, the kind she never had.

Maybe she should head back to Baltimore after seeing Mr. Avery and ditch all those ridiculous plans.

Want to read more? Get your copy of *LETHAL CAPERS*, the next installment of The Risky Changes Series on Amazon now!
If you enjoyed *Deadly Probabilities* please take a moment to leave an honest review for DL on Amazon!
Thank you!

OTHER BOOKS BY

DL Koontz

The Crossing series:

Crossing Into the Mystic
Edging Through the Darkness

Escaping the Abyss
What the Moon Saw

ABOUT THE AUTHOR

Degrees behind her, DL Koontz spent years in four glamorous cities hiding her early fiction ideas, first on journalists' notebooks where she detailed hard-news interviews, then on laptops as a management consultant and college instructor. She now lives with her husband in rural Georgia on a cattle ranch, where she divides her time between writing and endlessly "going to town" for supplies. Her debut novel, Crossing into the Mystic, was hailed as "a difficult book to put down," and touches everyone who has ever lost someone they love. She has been published in seven languages, and welcomes readers to her beautiful, crazy corner of the world where book lovers and optimists are welcome.

www.ingramcontent.com/pod-product-compliance
Lightning Source LLC
Chambersburg PA
CBHW030224180626
46810CB00008B/2962